Cover artwork by Shannon Cartier Lucy

shannoncartierlucy.bigcartel.

Interior by Joel Amat Güell

joelamatguell.com

Printed in the United States of America.

ISBN: 9781955904698

Published by CLASH Books, Troy, NY.

clashbooks.com

Earth Angel

Madeline Cash

Praise for Madeline Cash

"21 Books We're Most Excited About in 2023"

— Nylon

"[Cash] pushes her characters a step further than expected, hooks them up to an IV filled with irony, and watches as they degrade on their own slippery slopes."

—The Northwest Review

"Cash's stories are a reminder of what fiction can do when it's allowed to break the rules, express its moment, turn the despairing or the banal into something better."

—Compact

"Cash has created vibrant, sometimes nihilistic, often cuttingly hilarious vignettes, which you'll be hard pressed not to whizz through in one sitting."

—The Face

"The stories in *Earth Angel* are playful, charming, and a little bit devious—this is a striking debut by a writer to watch."

—Chelsea Hodson, author of *Tonight I'm Someone Else*

"*Earth Angel* is wonderfully vibrant and fresh. Madeline's stories are smart, hilarious, heartbreaking, and sharp. A glimmer of hope in the time of modern America."

—Petra Cortright, digital artist, *VVEB CAM 2007* currently exhibiting at MOMA

"Cash's heroines are all earth angels but none so much as presence in these stories of the author herself, whose style has a devilish (remember Satan was an angel) and celestial powers, quite apart from the characters and scenarios Cash has imagined."

—Christian Lorentzen, Bomb Magazine

"*Earth Angel* reiterates this sentiment: life is a hot mess, but we try to be happy. It's a fleeting happiness, ephemeral because something shitty will happen again—you'll see your rapist smiling on Instagram or be asked to do marketing copy for a terrorist organization—and you ultimately can't escape the great unknown, the black hole at the end of this book and everything else."

—LARB

"*Earth Angel* is vigorous, hilarious and demented. The nightmare of the now has a radiant and vicious new bard, and her name is Madeline Cash."

—Sam Lipsyte, author of *The Ask, Hark,* and *No One Left to Come Looking for You*

"The stories in her book are bizarre in the way that only a writer with her precision can employ."

—W Magazine

"...accelerated and fractured, closer to memes than Montaigne. She's so relentlessly funny, so manically inventive, that you might not at first notice the deep undercurrent of sadness beneath the scintillant surface..."

—Protégé, The Loaf with Tim Kreider

"I enjoyed Madeline's stories a lot. They're weird and funny and dead-pan, and they explore interesting, under-examined topics."

— Tao Lin, author of *Taipei* and *Leave Society*

"*Earth Angel* is a brutal, funny and dizzying fever dream of a book. Madeline Cash's stories read like the musings of a brilliant boarding school girl sucking on a DMT vape pen: an entire universe, vivid and writhing, is revealed beneath her placid stare. This is an electric debut."

— Nada Alic, author of *Bad Thoughts*

"Madeline Cash's short stories blaze through the Culture with supreme confidence, agility, and wit. Be it a plague of blood or sadistic fuckboy boyfriend or dog hitman, she continually doubles down on her premise, and again and again she wins. What a bold, promising debut by such a one-of-a-kind young writer."

— Harris Lahti, fiction editor at *Fence*

"I don't know what I can tell you about *Earth Angel*. In one way, it is the story of one million strong, beautiful, upper middle class women in modern America, and in another, truer way, it is an unhinged, joyous nosedive through every wild thought you've ever had played out real tender, like a movie. I love this book, please read it."

— Sasha Fletcher, author of *Be Here to Love Me at the End of the World*

"Madeline Cash twirls through the detritus of our ravaged modern age in her charming debut, *Earth Angel*. Armed with an electric humor, Cash spins glittering tales of a physical world in decline, a surveillance culture lit by glaring LEDs that is dispossessed and irreverent, having forgotten how heavy with meaning it is."

—Jen George, author of *The Babysitter at Rest*

"Raucously endearing, worldly but clear-souled, *Earth Angel* introduces an uncanny and crucial new voice. There isn't anything Madeline Cash doesn't know about the ruckussy graces of our present moment. I was laughing so hard, I didn't realize how fast my heart was breaking."

— Garielle Lutz, Author of *Worsted*

"If this is downtown Catholicism, this is its darkest, funniest, most nihilistic incarnation yet. The question of who—or what—is being skewered in these stories is an open one, but their sharpness is undeniable."

—Lindsay Lerman, author of *What Are You* and *I'm From Nowhere*

"*Earth Angel* is quotable, persuasive, glib, and profound—the compiled code of a lifetime spent amidst Hello Kitty sleeping bags, far-off forever wars, dying pets, sexual predators, and obsolescing handheld devices. It is a book as pleasurable, strange, and anxiety-provoking as (to use one of its own images) a Noah's Ark of Nintendogs. I loved it."

—Mark Doten, author of *Trump Sky Alpha*

"The mostly flash fiction that makes up this book are not quite magical realism so much as dream journals of a woman rapidly losing agency in a world increasingly dominated by universal surveillance, smartphone apps, and a technological complexity so advanced as to feel spiritual."

— Geoffrey Mak, author of *Mean Boys*, forthcoming from Bloomsbury in 2024

"The disconsolate souls of *Earth Angel* are crying out in the wilderness of modernity, aka greater Los Angeles, yearning—whether or not they know it—for grace to shatter their hyper-mediated, overmedicated, child-endangered, love-damaged lives. These stories are bleak, estranging, and bizarre; they're slyly profound, pretty sleazy, and funny as fuck. I'm reminded of my first encounters with such radical originals as Jen George, Dennis Cooper, Mark Doten, and Ariana Reines. To read Madeline Cash is to mainline her apocalyptic vitality, to witness a rare vision realized with an untamed sense of control, to light your cigarette off of the flames from her burning heart."

— Justin Taylor, author of *Riding With the Ghost*

Contents

Plagues 19

The Jester's Privilege 23

Slumber Party 41

They Ate The Children First 49

Hostage #4 59

Earth Angel 65

Beauty Queen 81

Sponge Cake 83

Mark's Turtles 87

TGIF 93

Little Dalmatia 97

Hollywood Tours 103

Fortune Teller 111

Water Sports 115

Good Boy 123

Little Dubrovnik 127

Autofiction 137

For mom and Ani

"I just wanted to show you cool animals!"

— Benjamin Mee, *We Bought A Zoo*

Plagues

FIRST IT WAS FROGS, then locusts, then remote aerial drone strikes. Clearly God was punishing us. God was punishing us but we were happy because at least we knew that God existed.

All the liquid turned to blood. The water in our Brita filters and the fountain at the mall—all blood. The bartenders balked as the gin and vodka ran red through their shakers. The men wouldn't stand for it. They blamed the women for the blood. The men blamed the women and the women blamed the horses and the horses blamed the babies and the babies cried for their milk which was blood, breast or bottle.

The frogs were getting out of hand. We dissected them in science class. The underserved communities were disproportionately affected by the frogs. If you were to kiss the frogs, they would not become princes. They'd chastise you for non-consensual touching. It was a disaster with PETA. Then the frogs started organizing. They formed an autonomous zone. They developed seasonal depression.

Everyone had a feeling that God had forsaken us. All the babies had colic. All the livestock had yeast infections. The rumor that God had forsaken us spread through our friends and neighbors and Priests. *God's forsaken us, pass it on.* In God's absence the girls rolled up their skirts. In God's absence we pierced our ears and sullied the purity of our flesh and bought crypto and wrote autofiction. We played truth or dare. Never have we ever. Marry fuck kill: Father, Son, and Holy Spirit. We abolished homosexual marriage and then heterosexual marriage and then marriage in general. The nuns, who were of course married to God, filed for divorce. They hired Jewish lawyers.

Madeline brought the lice. That one wasn't God. Madeline brought the lice from a boarding school in Vermont. Madeline passed the lice to Elijah who gave them to Anika who passed them to Jake Willner. Anika loved Jake Willner but Jake Willner could take it or leave it with Anika though Jake Willner would walk through hot coals for Katja who more or less hated Luca but loved Elijah who hung the moon for Abigail who passed the lice to Blake while giving him head in his parents' basement so we all had lice—though Blake only had genital lice. "The future is uncertain," said Elijah, "but we must keep on living so perhaps we should all make love in Blake's parents' basement." So we took shots of blood and scratched our collective hair and had group sex in the basement while frogs pelted the roof.

One day the sun went down and did not come back up. We used our phone flashlights to open our doors and put on our makeup and file our taxes and read our newspapers though luckily the newspapers were on our phones/flashlights. "Things have changed," said my mother, "since I was a girl." But we were happy. Because God existed. "Now sleep, sweet child, as we lie in wait for what horrors tomorrow may bring."

The Jester's Privilege

I CONCLUDE THIS WEEK'S VIRTUAL THERAPY session, like always, by lamenting my life's lack of meaning.

"I just wish I was doing something more noble with my time," I say.

"You don't find your work spiritually fulfilling?" asks my therapist.

I tell her no, I don't find my work spiritually fulfilling.

"Do you have a friend or colleague who does something that you feel is *noble*?"

"My friend Laura Cohen. She's in med school."

"And you consider this noble work?"

I don't know. I haven't spoken to Laura Cohen in three years. I assume, based on the number of social engagements she misses, that her work is spiritually fulfilling. Through the reflection of the screen in her glasses, I can see that my therapist is online shopping. I don't mind. Her services are covered by my insurance.

I live above a fish market in Chinatown. East Broadway smells like hot blood. Except in the winter when it smells like cold blood. You can buy anything in Chinatown like lobster or crab or squid or shark fin or PCP or a fake Burberry sun hat. I have never been to regular China. For breakfast I pop a handful of pistachios—a highly caloric nut—into my mouth, chew, then spit them out into a dish towel. Then I fill a dropper with 6ml of Metacalciquin intended to increase metabolism and shoot it down my throat. I do this every day. I find that it's best to do the same things every day to avoid decision fatigue. My vision blurs for about ten minutes, a common side-effect of the Metacalciquin, so I make my way to my desk by groping the walls.

I work for a marketing agency called Fresh Start. Our business has a focus on reputation laundering, which is to say, we take on clients who for one reason or another fell out of public favor and are looking for brand reinvention. The Fresh Start logo is an optical illusion or "ambiguous image." You might at first see a beetle, dead on its back, but turning your head reveals a phoenix rising from its ashes. We pioneer campaigns for the likes of Solomon handguns—*now with a smaller grip for kids!*, campaigns to reinstate Columbus Day, campaigns for dating apps with a focus on age-gap relationships, campaigns to lessen concern around the opioid crisis, campaigns for the Immigration and Customs Enforcement, ivory-poaching, crypto-fascism, factory farming, accused sexual predators, the recently incarcerated, puppy mills, fracking, lead-heavy paint companies. I have been working at Fresh Start for just under a year. For my anniversary, I hope they give me a new desk chair.

Xian texts me that he enjoyed our time together last night, which I assume is a formality. I met Xian on a dating app for young people living in ethnic diasporas out of financial necessity. He lives in Little Ethiopia. Yesterday was our third date. I thought he was taking me to the Met. Instead, he took me to a Stanford Prison Experiment themed escape room. We then held each other briefly outside of my apartment before amicably going our separate ways. I have not found much success in dating, which I attribute to a hormone or chemical lacking in my skin. Skin contact is incredibly important in intimate relationships—at least that is what I learned from *The Science of Intimacy*, although its writer, who also penned *The Science of Marketing*, has no discernible scientific background. I learned that there was a hormone or chemical lacking in my skin when a friend and I visited a spa in Mexico where you place your feet into a terrarium of small fish. I remember the proprietor kept referring to the fish as her little soldiers in Spanish. I watched as her little soldiers swarmed my friend's feet, eating small continents of dead skin off of her heels. But when it came to my turn, the fish did not eat my foot skin. They swam to either side of the tank, collectively affronted by the intrusion. "Maybe they're full," I had suggested, but the proprietor just looked disturbed.

I enter the "waiting room" for a video meeting with my boss, Dorian. While in the limbo of the video stall, I browse the internet and get a pop-up ad for a small defense lawyer. *If you or a loved one has taken Metacalciquin you are entitled to financial compensation.* I click the ad and skim its contents. *1 in 4 regular Metacalciquin users lose their sight permanently.* Dorian interrupts my reading with an overzealous hello. His enthusiasm for marketing is unparalleled. Dorian's video background depicts an apartment much nicer than his own, his silhouette disrupting its continuity when he gesticulates, which he does often. He tells me about a new docuseries that explores the social habits of field mice, the immense detail of his account quelling any need for me to watch it myself, had I the will to watch television. His video background changes to a beach in Malaysia. Or maybe Vietnam. Large, jagged mountains protruding from the digital water. I have never been to Malaysia or Vietnam.

"We have a super exciting new client BUT I am going to need you to come into the office for this one."

"We have an office?"

"We have an office!"

"Why do I need to come into the office for this one?"

"It's *so* not a big deal at all but I'm going to need you to sign a multilateral NDA."

Outside my window, I see a woman tending a fire in a metal trash bin, periodically sprinkling the flames with fake money. Sometimes they do this, my neighbors, as a way of sending wealth to their deceased in the next life. I wonder if the residents of this ethereal Chinatown notice that the currency isn't real. Perhaps fake money works in heaven.

On my way to the office, which evidently is and always has been south of Houston Street, I walk into a pizza shop and order the greasiest, most toppings-laden slice available. I eat it too quickly to detect any one specific flavor, then think about what I would take with me were my apartment to catch fire. My selections—laptop, passport—are out of convenience rather than sentimentality. I only have a brief window of time before the pizza digests irreversibly into my system so I induce vomiting outside a Polish church.

Dorian meets me at the door of the office and gives me an unsolicited tour. The office is in a restored factory with a cage elevator that shakes as it ascends. Dorian points out details in the crown molding. I realize that I have never seen the lower half of Dorian's body. In my eleven months at Fresh Start, we have never met or expressed any interest in meeting.

"This chandelier is from the 1490s," says Dorian.

"Doesn't look a day over 1460," I say.

"Ha!" says Dorian instead of laughing.

We settle into a large conference room. The walls are decorated with generic modern art. Muted swaths of color. Mass-produced Rorschach tests.

"What do you see when you look at this?" Dorian asks of the amorphous blobs.

"Amoebas," I lie.

"I see a slave ship on a choppy sea. Two lovers escaping religious persecution. A man castrating a horse." Dorian hands me the brief which is extensive and bound with brass fasteners.

"It's in Arabic," I say.

"That it is. That it is."

Dorian fans an NDA across the marble desk. It is also extensive. A non-disclosure novella.

"These folks are more sensitive so before we get into the nitty gritty…" Dorian produces a pen.

"I think I might need a lawyer."

"I *can* tell you this: the client wants an entire rebrand. Lots of opportunities for creative innovation." Dorian pushed up his sleeves to his elbows as though he was getting ready, physically, to create and innovate right here. "We're looking at an exclusive partnership."

"With whom?"

"Are you familiar with any jihadist rhetoric or the literal implementation of the Quran in general?"

"What are you talking about?"

Dorian checks over his shoulder. The office remains empty. "It's Islamic fundamentalism with a new flair." He spreads his fingers apart to make a little firework.

"Instilling the fear of God in a modern audience."

"I'm sorry, but…"

"Don't use an apology as a disclaimer. It's a subservient feminine quality and I like to think of us as equals."

"Dorian, I don't think we should get involved with the Islamic State."

"Why not? They want to *triple* our day rate. You just may need to cover your hair, nose, and mouth in future client meetings."

"It's objectively wrong."

"You're being a tad closed-minded."

"Am I though?"

"*You're* writing the narrative," says Dorian. "Wrong. Right. It's all fictional. It's whatever you make it."

I stare at the office art and, for a moment, I can see a horse. A sea.

"What is it that you think we do here?" asks Dorian.

"We're a creative marketing agency," I say.

"We're in the business of reality production," Dorian corrects me. "We don't tell people what to think. We tell people *how* to think." He's getting animated in his motion now. Gesturing more. Blinking less. "Guy Debord—are you familiar with this fellow? He's really worth a Google!— Debord said, 'I wanted to speak the beautiful language of my century.' Do you know what that language is?"

"French?"

"Advertising! We are speaking the language of the consumer. We're waxing poetic to the everyman. We don't just supply content to hedge fund managers and South American war lords. We are the premier gateway between truth and individual." He pats the backs of two chairs, as though *truth* and *individual* are currently in the room with us.

"Marketing is the bedrock of late capitalism. As a junior strategist, you are the arbiter of twenty-first-century America. You hold the keys to an empire, albeit a smaller empire than say my empire but an empire nonetheless. What do you want to do with those keys?" Dorian makes a pyramid with his thumbs and pointer fingers.

I tell him I am going to need the rest of the day to think.

When I get back to Chinatown, Xian is waiting outside of my apartment. This would constitute our fourth date though we did not have previous arrangements to get together and this spontaneity prickles me. Not a bad prickle. The way I can only imagine it might feel to have one's feet nibbled by fish at a Mexican spa. Xian unpacks a bag of groceries and says he is going to make gratin dauphinois. I don't know what gratin dauphinois is but I know that I will need a suite of vitamins to help me digest it. I catch Xian staring at my winter boots.

"It's odd," says Xian, "that you wear leather but don't eat meat."

I tell him that my vegetarianism is not moral but dietary.

"I understand that nihilism is in vogue for your generation"—Xian delineates between my generation and his as he is seven years older—"but there must be something you find meaningful?"

"What do you find meaningful?" I ask.

"God, French cooking, the way the sky changes from summer to fall."

As Xian cooks, I excuse myself to the bathroom and call Laura Cohen at the New York Presbyterian School for Medicine and Medical Research. I ask her if she has ever been out in a public setting, say a cafe or train station, and witnessed someone collapse as a stranger yells, "Is anyone a doctor?" and has she, Laura Cohen, gone to their aid?

"No, thank G-d," says Laura Cohen. "I don't think that happens as much as you might think."

"What's new?" I ask.

"Not much. There are microscopic shellfish in the New York City tap water," she says.

"That seems like it should be a bigger problem for the kosher community," I say.

Then I ask Laura Cohen if she is spiritually fulfilled.

"I guess," she says. "I gave a late-term abortion to a woman in Buffalo last week."

I sense Xian listening at the door so I turn on the faucet.

"So, what are you doing these days?" Laura Cohen asks

me.

I tell her that I'm the arbiter of twenty-first-century America.

"That's cool. Well, nice catching up with you." Laura Cohen hangs up and I stare at the water as it pools in the sink, inspecting for tiny shellfish.

I wake up to the distinct clang of a Chinese funeral procession headed down the block. This happens about once a week. Xian is asleep next to me, still wearing the clothes in which he arrived. I climb onto my fire escape and watch the grieving men and women plod solemnly down East Broadway. Listen to their melancholic instruments being blown and strummed and picked. Little children carry whimsical flags after the casket. Xian stirs, comes to the window and looks at me.

"Are you crying?" he asks.

"Oh," I say. "I guess so."

"You came back," says Dorian when I come back.

"I knew you'd come back."

"It was touch and go there for a while."

"Come in. I just ordered coffee. Can't figure out this machine! Too many bells and whistles in my opinion." Dorian glares at a twelve-hundred-dollar espresso machine. I dawdle in the mouth of the elevator. It occurs to me that we are the only two people in the office for a second day in a row and I begin to wonder if anyone else works for Fresh Start.

"I have some stipulations," I say, "for the direction of

the campaign."

Dorian smiles and ushers me inside. Despite the office being empty, he shuts the conference room door behind us.

"Alright," he says. "Pitch me."

"What do religious extremists in their early twenties have that we don't have?" I ask.

"Less pre-marital sex?"

"Something to believe in."

Dorian nods, sage-like.

"If we're going to make terrorism palatable to a contemporary market, we're going to need to shift the discourse a little. I've added some tenets to the brief."

"Body-positivity. Climate consciousness. Gender-affirming," Dorian reads aloud. "Monthly donations to the Anti-Defamation League?"

"And triple my day rate," I confirm.

"You want to incorporate the ideology of neoliberalism into Sunni Islam."

"This is, as they say, my hard line."

"I like to see you taking some agency," says Dorian.

He lays out the NDA.

"Daniel Ortega—a client of ours!—once said to me, 'you go to sleep with the boys, you wake up with the men.' A funny line from someone actively trying to discourage homosexual accusations but I think it applies here."

He plucks a pen from his jacket pocket.

"Are you ready to wake up with the men?"

I sign the papers, relinquishing my right to share any details of our work on the project digitally, verbally, or otherwise.

Dorian takes me out to celebrate. To get to the bar of his choosing, we must walk through a travel agency which is in the back of a nail salon which is in the back of an underground mall. The room is dark and smokey and music pulses from within. Dorian orders two shots that come on fire. His whitened teeth glow in the darkness. I briefly imagine Dorian murdering me, standing over my prone body with that same unflinching smile. I try to text Xian but there is no service.

"No service," says Dorian. "That's why it's called Off the Grid. Isn't that fun?"

"Really fun," I say.

"Let's make idle chit-chat. What are your hobbies? Do you have love in your life?" Dorian asks. "I'm not being fresh, by the way. If you can't tell by my attire or vocal affect, I am unflinchingly gay. My boyfriend's a psychopharmacologist. Pablo."

"Doesn't it make you feel bad," I ask. "The work that we do?"

"Why would it?"

"Isn't it contradictory to what I assume, as a gay socialist, are your core values?"

"I'm not going to sit here and tell you that right or wrong have any purchase in the greater scheme of things." Dorian takes his shot. "Do you know what it was like growing up in Durham, North Carolina? They used to run up to my dad and sing '*don't let your son go down on me*' to the tune of—"

"No, yeah I get it."

"My primary assailant was a kid called Tadam Biddle. Do you know what Tadam is doing now?"

"What is Tadam doing now?"

"He made a fortune in crypto. Lives on a houseboat."

I stare at Dorian or the teeth that are Dorian in this bar. Noting my lack of enthusiasm for the drink, he downs my flaming shot. I am not a big drinker because alcohol is highly caloric and causes a significant disruption to my routine. I ask for a glass of water and Dorian orders another drink.

"It doesn't matter," says Dorian. "We're all the same," his voice slurring with imminent inebriation.

"And I don't say that fatalistically, I take comfort in it. You, me, Tadam Biddle," he gestures outward, vaguely towards the streets of Lower Manhattan. "Working stiffs, housewives, schoolchildren, church-goers, the upper class and middle class and—what are they calling it now?— working class, but then more specifically widows and illegal immigrants, truckers and people with master's degrees, drifters, retired landowners, sovereign citizens, teamsters, the mentally insane, ambulance chasers, girlbosses, teachers and nurses, protesters, Southern aristocrats, temps, sex workers, Satanists, the young and beautiful, intravenous drug users, the people who stand outside of art galleries, industry plants, Canadian jocks, rust belters, foreign heirs, Hasids, carnies, plastic surgeons, men with Napoleon complexes, engineers, podcasters, the terminally ill, Holocaust deniers, terrorists, kings and queens, in the monarchical sense not the colloquial one. All the same."

"What are you?" I ask.

"Easy," says Dorian. "I'm the jester. My societal role allows me to speak truth to power. I'd say you are too but you don't seem to participate in enough self-parody."

"I can make fun of myself."

"Alright, then you're the jester too. Cheers, jester."

Dorian clinks his drink with my water glass which the more superstitious consider to be bad luck.

The weeks slip into months fluidly as I focus on my "work-life balance." Xian and I continue to see each other. I once heard or read, though I have long forgotten where, that your time alone prepares you for the time when you have love in your life. I try to reflect on my time alone but cannot draw any conclusions from my past. Like receiving fake money in the next life, it's of no use to me here. Xian doesn't seem to sense the missing chemical in my skin. We have been intimate now, including several ways that cannot lead to procreation so I know that his motives for being with me are more than purely biological. I have gone out with Dorian and his psychopharmacologist boyfriend Pablo on several occasions and to several inconveniently located but no doubt upwardly trending bars. On Tuesdays I play mahjong with my downstairs neighbor. The game is complicated, almost intentionally so, but I am learning quickly and I like how the little tiles feel in my palm.

The increase in my day rate has allowed me to employ a better therapist and purchase a new desk chair. I once read that even the subtle improvement to one's daily posture has immeasurable effects on one's mood. I assume these immeasurable effects are positive. I also bought a weekend getaway to the Poconos with which I plan to surprise Xian since he seems to have a penchant for spontaneity. I have this daydream, this fantasy, that we will spot a little house in the country, dilapidated—reflected in the price—but charming, a "fixer-upper." We'll purchase the house and live out our days somewhere rural and in close proximity to a stream. Then, if I entertain these fantasies long enough, I win a prize for ethical marketing. Xian opens a restaurant, Parisian-Pennsylvanian fusion. We will feel a sense of great peace.

One evening, while Xian is preparing a Roux ("the basis for all French cuisine!") I dial my soon-to-be-doctor friend Laura Cohen. I tell her that I miss her. I tell her that I have made improvements to my posture and am entertaining a sense of great peace. I tell her that I have been seeing someone and he's currently in my kitchen making a Roux. Laura Cohen says that she's happy for me. She says that she too is seeing someone, engaged to him actually. He's also a doctor from a long line of doctors and his family is throwing them an engagement party at the Plaza on Saturday and I may attend if I like.

Dorian calls me early on a Saturday. At first, the call incorporates into my dream. It's a Chinese funeral procession. The instruments are spouting my ringtone.

"Buenos días! Why are you whispering?"

I tell Dorian that I am whispering as to not wake Xian who sleeps next to me on his back like a sarcophagus.

"I'm calling from Mexico City. Roma Norte! Pablo and I adore it here and have decided…we're going to stay! We're seeing the cutest house this afternoon. Colonial revival. And the price of living—"

"You're moving to Mexico?"

"Si! And, considering the time difference, I will of course be handing in my resignation to Fresh Start. When asked whom I might want to succeed me, I might have dropped your name. All of our clients are so taken with you, it shouldn't be a problem."

"What are you talking about?"

"Did I stutter? I'm genuinely asking. I've had quite a bit to drink already."

"You're quitting the agency and moving to Mexico."

"The keys to the empire are yours, Jester. If you want them."

Dorian hangs up and Xian shifts in his sleep next to me, instinctively moving closer to my body which, as I've said, does not repel him.

The grandiose lobby of the Plaza Hotel reminds me of Versailles or the Kremlin. This comparison, of course, I am basing off of depictions because I've never been to France or Russia. But soon, I will have been to the Poconos. Making my way into the Tea Room I see Laura Cohen, surrounded by twenty or so doctors and their respective spouses, sitting next to a nebbish young man who is presumably her husband-to-be.

I settle on one of the quips I plan on using to open conversation.

"I hear the third leading cause of death in America is medical malpractice," I say.

"What?" says Laura Cohen.

"It's good to see you and congratulations." I hand her a pink box.

"They're macarons. I got them in the lobby gift shop."

"Thanks. Yeah, it's wild."

"Laura..?"

"Oh, his last name is also Cohen."

"Are you sure you're not related?"

"Yeah, we checked. Do you want to meet him? Felix—" She taps the man next to her. He's performing surgery on a caviar-topped tartlet with a little silver spoon. We shake hands and he offers me a glass of champagne. I pretend to sip it out of habit and then actually sip it and the liquid warms my entire body.

Felix stands and is so soft-spoken that at first I don't even realize he is delivering a speech.

"My heart, it's no longer my own. Perhaps I'll pivot into cardiology to better understand how she did it. Doctors, practical people that we are, like to make sense of things. We take comfort in organization, regime, strategy, etc. But at the end, and I have seen people at the end, crossing over into the next leg of their journey—I apologize for the morbid turn this has taken—but see, at the end, little else matters except, well. Love has helped me see beauty in senselessness. I'd marry you a thousand times Laura Cohen—to whom I am not even distantly related [pauses for laughter]. And even though I have palpated 3 different rectums today, you would be hard pressed to find a luckier man alive."

Everyone in the vicinity raises a glass.

"Congrats to you both," I say and stand to take my leave.

"Thanks for coming," says Laura Cohen. "And it's cool you got that terrorist organization to participate in affirmative action or whatever. They seem to be doing a lot of great work for the community. That was you right?"

I mime zipping my mouth shut and head out of the Tea Room. A clatter of glass and silverware draws the party's attention to a table over where an old man has collapsed.

THE JESTER'S PRIVILEGE

He's choking, perhaps on a cucumber sandwich or mille-feuille. His distressed dining mate, an elegantly dressed and significantly younger woman screeches, "Is anyone a doctor?" Everyone at Felix and Laura Cohen's table stands. I make my way to the foyer and out the revolving door.

Slumber Party

~~~~~~~~~~~~~~~~~~~~~~~~~~~~~~~~~~~~~~~

ON THE EVE OF MY THIRTIETH BIRTHDAY, I decide to host a slumber party. I inflate air mattresses and pop popcorn and rent a log cabin in the woods, which will lend the perfect backdrop for scary storytelling. I call my very best friend in the world. My very best friend in the world tells me she's nine months pregnant, going into labor as we speak actually, and can't make it to my slumber party. I say I understand and ask that she at least name the baby after me, even a middle name would suffice, to which she says *no* and does not wish me a happy birthday. I call my second- and third-best friends. My second-best friend tells me that she moved to Dubai six years ago for work, and my third-best friend is planning her flash mob wedding, rendering her unavailable. I call my work colleague. My work colleague says she thinks it would be uncomfortable for us to spend any amount of time together outside of work, even a lunch, and that it would be more appropriate for me to invite a best friend or very best friend. I call my upstairs neighbor. The police answer and inform me that my upstairs neighbor was murdered during a violent break-in by that killer, the one who targets women in their early thirties. I offer my condolences.

I drive to the log cabin in the woods to meet Max and Walker and Zoe. I rented them on Slumberparty LLC through the Childhood Memories app. They arrive with supplies like healing mud masks and energy drinks and tarot cards and an eighth of cocaine and new iPhone minis and a PS7, which will all be charged to my credit card on file. I worry it might be awkward at first but the actors are very professional. Zoe even brought an itinerary:

5 p.m. Cocktails
6 p.m. Karaoke
7 p.m. Practice Altruism
8 p.m. Gossip
9 p.m. Mani/pedi
10 p.m. ASL
11 p.m. Prank calls
12 a.m. Group sex
1 a.m. Mine Bitcoin/build blockchain
2 a.m. Binge/purge
3 a.m. Conjure the dead
4 a.m. Network
5 a.m. Freeze our eggs

"We want you to have the classic slumber party experience," explains Zoe. We all must sing *House of the Rising Sun* for karaoke. I ask if we can order lox and bagels in the morning but Anika tells me that lox and bagels are a high-caloric food and I did not select the traditional Semitic breakfast section in the Childhood Memories app. I ask when we can tell scary stories and she says life is the scary story. Then we watch forty-five minutes of *Shoah*.

For Altruism at 7 p.m. Zoe uses my card on file to clean up an oil spill in the Mediterranean. Max and Walker buy Pelotons for underserved communities. "And so we beat on," says Zoe. She tells me to pick a cause: women, gays, rust belt families poisoned by the water supply, the ice caps, pygmy goats, Fortune 500 CEOs on house arrest, victims of whiplash, older tennis players, Texans in the winter, the Taliban in the springtime, Roe v. Wade, garden-variety voter suppression. I decide to bail someone out of prison. It ends up being my upstairs neighbor's murderer.

Zoe cups her hand to my ear. I like how her warm breath feels on my skin. These moments of closeness are what it is to be human. It's time to gossip. She tells me that Max has fetal alcohol syndrome and that Walker has several offshore bank accounts and that Amazon is behind Brexit and that God is dead and that babies can see a litany of colors that we can't even register. I tell her that I'd like to have a baby one day. "Motherhood will give me purpose," I say. Zoe paints a Chinese dragon on my toenails.

At 10 p.m. we start learning ASL. "I've never had a real sleepover before," I admit. "Is this part of the classic slumber party experience?" "No!" Zoe signs. But the app is sponsored by the American Sign Language Association so we must comply. I sign that I just want to reiterate how grateful I am to have them all over and that it really feels like I'm among friends and that these are the formative moments I'll remember in life and, even though it's their job, I hope this night is extra special for them as well. They pretend not to understand me.

The boys make prank calls asking if the recipient's refrigerator is running. I imagine a refrigerator running—really running, in a 10k with condiments flying left and right—and laugh to myself. This kind of whimsy is what will make me a good mother.

At midnight I am instructed to strip. I shed my footie pajamas, which Zoe promptly throws into the fireplace. Zoe initiates the group sex by fucking Walker as he sucks off Max who whispers something in my ear. He says he can tell my star sign by the texture of my cervical mucus. He's sexually clairvoyant. He sticks his fingers inside me and says, "Gemini rising." They play a club remix of *House of the Rising Sun*.

I find myself hoping that Zoe will open up to me, tell me about her family, or want to do something called a fish braid to my hair. But she remains in character. Contractually obligated stoicism. I think, if we'd met under different circumstances, Zoe might be a second—or even a first—best friend.

I take notes as Max and Walker explain decentralized currency. They say the Dow is up. The Jones is down. "Bull market," they say. "Liquidity. Mutual funds. Bid-ask spread. Standard deviation. Dividends. Buyback," they say. "Volatility?" I say. "Price-return? Fifty two-week high? Blue chip? Benchmark?" I ask. "Good point," they agree.

While the boys play video games, Zoe takes me to TheSaladBar in town. They know her at TheSaladBar and on her 280th visit they'll give her free dressing. We order massive salads and mine comes with a candle for my birthday. Zoe tells me to make a wish as she signs my name on the check. "I wish to have a real slumber party by my 40th. With a husband and kids and friends and their husbands and their kids." I blow out the salad candle. The waiter looks at me with pity.

Next thing I know, we're back in the log cabin and Zoe is retching green bile into the toilet. I don't think the old plumbing can handle it. I hold her hair and pat her back. I feel maternal towards her. She tells me that it's my turn next and I say I don't want to. This doesn't feel like the classic slumber party experience. She tells me that Childhood Memories prides itself on its accuracy. I refuse to vomit and Zoe, or the actor who plays Zoe, looks angry with me. "Grow up," she says.

Outside the bathroom, the boys have prepared a seance. They wear brown hooded robes and burn palo santo and have a virgin tied up in the corner. I wave *hi* to the virgin and she signs happy birthday back to me in ASL. She asks me how old I'm turning and I hold up *three zero* and she turns away disturbed. Max takes a vial of the virgin's blood and pours it over Zoe's leftovers from TheSaladBar. "It's time for you to communicate with the dead," they say. I kneel in front of the takeout container and wonder who will be conjured. I hope it's the boy from summer camp who everyone called a faggot and then drowned in the lake. I hope I can apologize to him and assure him that growing up isn't that great and ask what the afterlife is like. But when the specter appears it's not the boy from summer camp but my grandmother's Cocker Spaniel who peed in my violin case. The ghost dog gnashes its teeth at me and growls. Max says it reflects negatively on my character to be so disliked by animals. "You'll never get into heaven," barks the Cocker Spaniel. It prances over and licks the virgin's face affectionately.

I tell everyone that I want to go to bed. Max hands me an iPhone mini and says it's not time for sleeping. It's time for networking. He also hands me a script: *It's been too long // How are _____ and _____ // We have to get out to the Cape more // I did want to talk to you about something specific actually // I have a mutually beneficial opportunity // I thought of you immediately.* Max and Walker and Anika don headsets for more fluid, hands-free communication and do lines of Adderall as they network. My grandmother's dead dog and the virgin escape into the woods. I suddenly feel very alone. I open the Childhood Memories app's rate-your-experience survey offering: "epic" or "meh." I select "meh."

Zoe says it's time to freeze our eggs. I say I've always imagined having a family the old-fashioned way. She says, "I'm not paid to indulge in pipe dreams. I'm paid to facilitate the classic slumber party experience which entails understanding our limits as people. You probably won't find the perfect husband at your age but you could have the perfect child basted into your uterus." "I've been considering adoption," I tell Zoe. Zoe says that adopted kids are always weird and maladjusted. I tell her that I was adopted. She says that the medical fee for our egg freezing was already charged and is non-refundable. She suggests I do something to fill out my body. Perhaps lip injections or breast implants.

Max and Walker come into my bedroom with crowbars as the sun starts to rise. They say that they noticed I checked "meh" when rating my experience and if I don't check "epic" immediately they will break both of my kneecaps. I change my experience to "epic." They leave without saying goodbye. The palo santo sparks have started a fire in the living room and the log cabin is filling with smoke. I gather my things and tip Zoe extra because she makes 15 percent less than Max and Walker. I ask her again if she wants to exchange email addresses or something. The sparks have spread to the surrounding woodlands and a forest fire is now raging. Helicopters begin dropping water from above. Zoe says maybe she'll see me on my fortieth birthday and gets into the Slumberparty van which is parked outside. I use the forest fire to light a cigarette and walk two hundred miles back to my apartment.

My apartment door is open when I get home. The lock has been picked and the deadbolt stolen. I assume my upstairs neighbor's murderer had come looking for me and will surely be back. I google burial plots. I can't afford them after what I spent on Slumberparty LLC. I call my very best friend in the world and ask if she'll attend my funeral. She tells me she's experiencing a reverse postpartum after having her baby the old-fashioned way and is filled with constant euphoria. She's far too elated to reflect on my short, morbid life. "But not that short," she reminds me. She and her husband begin making love and forget to hang up. I listen for a while.

An unknown number calls on the other line and I answer. It's Zoe's voice asking if my refrigerator is running. I go to my refrigerator and open it. Every shelf is filled with lox and bagels. There are also capers and lemons and a petri dish of frozen embryos. I open the petri dish and the embryos are squirming. They move like inchworms, then like jumping beans—ricocheting out of their container and into the living room. They begin sprouting arms and legs. They're in the throes of evolution. They're plasma, then protozoa, then babies in bonnets. I try to breastfeed them but they've grown again, into toddlers then into petulant tweens and they're eating all the bagels. Then they're in graduation caps. They're moving the tassel from right to left. "They grow up so fast," I say as they pack their bags for college. "We love you mom," say the embryos, hugging me as I cry and remind them to call. I realize I'm still holding my phone. I thank Zoe. *House of the Rising Sun* plays through the receiver.

They Ate The Children First

NICK AND I SAT ON THE PORCH watching our neighbors fight in the street. The girl neighbor was hitting the guy neighbor with her flip-flop. She was barefoot and wearing a bikini top. The couple had been squatting in the condemned house down the block. Sometimes I wanted to hit Nick with a flip-flop. But not that night. That night we were sitting on the porch. The baby was on my lap. I held her up to eye level. "I don't think she's mine," I said to Nick. Nick said, "Well I saw her come out of you." I said I wanted a DNA test. Nick said she kind of looked like Howard Stern and we went on like that. I finished my glass of wine and Nick made a remark about my drinking. I reminded him that I wasn't nursing. I wasn't nursing because the baby wouldn't latch onto my nipples which I took offense to initially. Then it was quiet until the baby burst out laughing. Uncontrollably. Everything was funny to her; Nick was funny, the neighbors' domestic violence was funny, her own laughter—funniest of all.

I started grinding my teeth. Insurance didn't cover much by way of dental so I went to a cheap place in the Valley to get fitted for a mouth guard. I came home and told Nick about the cheap place in the Valley and how it smelled like cigarettes and how the posters were all yellowed and curling but Nick did not find my anecdotes endearing. Nick took my anecdotes as criticism of the life he'd provided for the baby and me. I said I loved the life he'd provided for the baby and me. Then he put on the harness and strapped the baby to his chest like a suicide bomb and went for a walk.

My teeth-grinding got worse and started giving me headaches. I called the cheap dentist in the Valley to check on the status of my mouth guard and the receptionist who picked up said that the practice was shutting down because the dentist had died. I said I was sorry and asked what had happened and she told me that the dentist had killed himself. I said. "Jesus. I must have been one of his last patients," and the receptionist said, "yeah, actually."

On April 1st I decided to surprise Nick with a prank. I strapped the baby into the baby vest and went to Petco. The sales clerk at Petco had no problem selling me a goldfish because I had a baby strapped to my chest which meant I probably didn't abuse animals. I hadn't fancied myself an animal abuser either. The prank was simple: Nick drank a lot of water. He kept a large jug of water by the bed and guzzled it every couple of minutes. I decided that I'd put a goldfish in the water jug so that when he went to guzzle the jug he'd see it now contained a goldfish and we'd both have a laugh and stay together forever. But what happened instead was: I put the fish in the jug and Nick went to guzzle it rather absent-mindedly and the fish came cascading out onto his face before I could say, "wait!" and it went flopping around on the comforter, traumatizing Nick more than pranking him. We got the fish into some new water but the PH was wrong so it died anyway. All the commotion got the baby crying and Nick bounced the baby as he lectured me like, "How can you still be so immature? You're about to turn [REDACTED]." And I explained that I hadn't meant to pelt Nick with the fish but, in fact, intended to strengthen our relationship. Nick said, "You need to grow up. We have a kid," and went on like that and I ground my teeth into plateaus.

The neighbors were at it again. The girl neighbor launched limes at the guy neighbor from the lime tree. She was wearing her bikini top and I wondered if the condemned house had a pool or something. Nick read the newspaper and sipped his coffee. The newspaper was on his phone. I asked what he was reading. He said he was reading an article about a plane crash in the Himalayas. The people were stranded for a long time and started eating each other. It was systematic. They ate the children first because the children were least likely to survive. Then a rescue mission came and saved them and all the survivors had to live with the fact that they'd eaten the children. "Jesus," I said. The baby looked at us skeptically from her baby pen.

I was getting the feeling that Nick was going to leave me. The baby wouldn't latch onto my nipples and I sensed that Nick sensed that I was a failed writer and a phony parent and a functional alcoholic. I googled things that bond people. Google said *trauma*. There were stories of army buddies perennially bonded with one another. I noted that Nick and I could not go to war. We were both out of shape and had the baby and I didn't think there was a war going on anyway. Google said *shared experiences bond people*. I googled *life-changing experiences*. There were a lot of articles about Jesus. There were articles about heroin. There were articles about seeing the Northern Lights and surviving cancer and joining NXIVM and reading Faulkner. I found an article about a popular research chemical called 2CX. It was a dopamine enhancer and an animal sedative used in small doses to cure schizophrenia and hair loss and aging. People who took it recounted hearing angels singing. They reconnected with their high school sweethearts and rekindled their marriages. Some spoke to God or accidentally swallowed their tongues or finished the Sunday crossword. Though it wasn't FDA-approved it was very unlikely to kill you. It caused some eyeball swelling. That didn't seem so bad. I didn't want to read Faulkner.

"Have you heard about 2CX?" I asked Nick. Nick made a noise like he was not listening to me. He didn't look up from the newspaper. I said I thought we should try it that weekend for our anniversary while Nick's mom had the baby. Nick said he'd pick some up at Sprouts later. "I'm serious," I said. Nick said we were too old to smoke some new drug. I said you didn't smoke it so much as dabbed it into your eyes with a dropper. He asked me why we would want to dab something into our eyes and I said because I felt like we were fading away. I said he looked at me differently. I said our relationship needed a little *je ne sais quoi* and I thought that *je ne sais quoi* might be this research chemical I read about online. I said it evoked passion and pastel hallucinations and he sighed. He asked how long it lasted because he was going to the driving range on Sunday. I said he should be fine by then.

The girl neighbor was tanning in a lawn chair outside the condemned house. I walked up to her with the baby in the baby vest. I was wearing the baby vest backwards so it was more like a baby backpack. I said "hey" to the girl neighbor and something about how it was such a nice day, one in a series of nice days, and she looked at me like I was a cop. The guy neighbor was working on a car. He was making a lot of banging noises and swearing.

I said, "men."

She said, "right." Then she said, "is that your kid?"

And I said, "yeah."

She said, "kind of looks like Howard Stern."

I said, "I know." Then I said, "do you know where I could buy some 2CX?"

She said, "excuse me?" but not like she didn't hear me. Like I'd insulted her.

I said, "it's a research chemical."

She said, "I know what it is."

I said, "it's for my anniversary."

She said, "are you serious?"

I said, "I have money."

The girl neighbor didn't say anything but took out an

iPhone from the 1800s and texted for a while. "What about your friend here?" she said about the baby. I said that the baby was sober. Then I quickly amended my statement to say that the baby would be staying at her grandmother's over the weekend. The girl neighbor told me I could meet someone in Lancaster that night who would hook me up. Then she looked at me like I was the stupidest person she'd ever met in her entire life and went back inside the condemned house.

"That's what you're wearing to buy drugs?" I asked Nick. He asked what was wrong with what he was wearing to buy drugs and I said he looked like an HR representative. Nick wasn't on board with the 2CX plan even after I told him that it only caused homicidal tendencies in less than 1% of users. But he said he'd come with me to Lancaster so that I didn't get murdered. I said that if we both got murdered then the baby would be an orphan. He said we'd have to bring the baby too so that way we would all get murdered. And then we'd just be gone. Like those children in the plane crash. Like my dentist. So we decided to bring the baby. Plus the baby liked car rides.

In the car, Nick told me that Lancaster is known for its Chinese food. I asked why and he said because a lot of Chinese families settled there and I asked why and he said he didn't know why. I noted that Lancaster had very little geographic similarity to China. Or at least not the Chinese landscapes I'd seen pictured in screensavers; green, mountainous. Lancaster was mostly desert with a few outlet malls. The sun set. The baby was asleep in her car seat. She loved car rides. She loved everything. Except my nipples. After we'd been driving for about 45 minutes the car GPS told us to turn down a road where we'd meet someone to sell us some 2CX. The girl neighbor had told me to bring $500 cash and I had said that seemed kind of steep and she said "inflation" and shrugged. So we had $500 cash. We passed a billboard for a new movie about the Himalayan plane crash. We drove until the road dead-ended at some train tracks. My heart was pounding and I could tell Nick's was too. He kept playing drums on the steering wheel. "I love you," I said and he said he did too. He killed the headlights and it was dark.

Nick lit the flashlight on his phone. We strapped the baby to his chest and walked down the train tracks for about half a mile as instructed. He took my hand. We were more in love already. Eventually a silhouette appeared from behind an idle freight train and walked towards us. As the silhouette got closer I could see that it was the guy neighbor. Nick shined the phone flashlight at him. His eyes were red and engorged and his pupils were floating listlessly like the triangle center in a shaken magic 8-ball. "Put that fucking light out," he said. Nick turned off the flashlight. It took our eyes a moment to adjust and take in what was going on. What was going on was the guy neighbor had pulled a gun on us. He told us to empty our pockets. Nick and I put our hands up even though he hadn't instructed us to. The guy neighbor noticed the baby in the baby vest. "Are you two retarded? Why would you bring a baby here?" he asked. I said respectfully that we hadn't anticipated things unfolding this way. He said, "I'd never bring my kid to a place like this" and I wondered if he meant that he would never bring his kid to buy drugs or to Lancaster in general.

I hadn't realized that the neighbors had a baby at all. I wondered if, under different circumstances, our respective children would have played together.

The guy neighbor spat into the gravel. Nick and I slowly emptied our pockets and tossed their contents at his feet: our phones and wallets, the $500 cash and the car keys, a pacifier. The baby cooed. She loved the guy neighbor. She loved everything. Then my phone started ringing on the ground. The ringing startled the guy neighbor and he shot my phone and the ringing stopped. The gunshot made the baby laugh. Uncontrollably. She'd be slapping her knee if her limbs had that kind of autonomy. Smoke rose from my phone screen. "Did you tell anyone you were coming here?" shouted the guy neighbor and we said "no." He told us to get on our knees and face the other direction. I wondered if he would shoot us despite the baby. If Nick would die in that outfit. I wondered how long it would take the Lancaster PD to find us out here. I wondered if we'd be on the news and if I'd become posthumously famous. If the short stories I wrote in college would gain notoriety. Nick's colleagues would absorb his clients. My friends would post photos of me online with morose captions. People would look at the photos and say, "They were so young." They'd say, "I heard they were having marital problems." They'd say, "That baby looks like Howard Stern." And then we'd just be gone. The baby tired herself out from laughing and it got quiet. It was a nice night. It was one in a series of nice nights.

We were on our knees on the ground in Lancaster. It didn't look anything like China. I peeked over my shoulder at the guy neighbor who still had the gun pointed at our backs. I wondered if he was having pastel hallucinations. He said, "You two are the dumbest motherfuckers I've ever met," and started walking back the way we came. I thought about the neighbors' teamwork involved in orchestrating this plan. They would never bring their baby to a place like this. They would never eat the children first. They might have been the perfect couple. I didn't share this insight with Nick because we had just been robbed. We waited for a few moments and listened to the guy neighbor's footsteps on gravel get further and further away. Then we stood up. By the time we reached the road, our car was gone. It was a lease. I thought of the car seat in the back.

We walked forever. Nick didn't speak to me as we walked. I strapped on the baby because Nick was shaking and it was making her fussy. She weighed a ton. I noted that she must be obese and we should call a doctor. I wondered if our insurance would cover diet baby formula. We walked until we found one of the good Chinese restaurants and asked to use their phone. We waited for Nick's mom to come get us like a couple of teenagers. The restaurant owner gave us some soup. He waved at the baby. She loved him. We said we'd been robbed but he looked at us knowingly. I wondered if he had any 2CX. I wondered if Nick would divorce me. Nick put his head in his hands. In the car there was a lot of, "How can you be so careless? You're about to turn [REDACTED]." And, "You need to grow up. You are parents now. How could you put the baby in this type of situation." And then a lot of silence. When we got home, the neighbors had cleared out of the condemned house and the car seat was on our lawn.

Hostage #4

I'M THIRTEEN AND I LOOK LIKE A CHILD BRIDE in my Confirmation dress. I receive the sacrament from an old pastor who's also my math teacher and it's titillating the way he grazes my tongue with the wafer. I hoard quarters to play Dance Dance Revolution at the arcade after school and my feet fly over the neon arrows. I'm on level: EXPERT and I'm so good that I have to lean back on the bar for support. My friends are on Animal Crossing and Club Penguin and have Nintendogs and Neopets and Tamagotchis and all of the simulated animals of 2008 and the US is in a financial crisis and I'm reading a book called TTYL by Lauren Myracle which is the pinnacle of literature as far as I'm concerned. The pastor tells me to read the Bible which is not written by Lauren Myracle. I imagine Noah's Ark filled with Nintendogs.

My Lutheran middle school is putting on a theatrical reenactment of the Iranian Hostage Crisis to teach us about modern secularism. It's directed by Mr. Hayworth who everyone calls Mr. Gayworth until he actually leaves his wife for a man and they move to Missoula. In the play, I get cast as Hostage #4 and I spend afternoons with my crush Dante who smells like asphalt and Fun Dip and it's titillating. I'm IM-ing with Dante and he asks me to take something off and then he'll take something off, that's the game, but I'm too shy to take something off so Dante calls me a virgin and blocks me. I roll up my uniform skirt to make it shorter and get detention and I practice cello in detention which makes me hate the cello and I probably could have been a first-chair concert cellist had they just let me wear my skirt above the knee like an American but now I forever associate cello with punishment and rejection and stop playing and start stealing cigarettes from my mom's friend Lisa's purse and sneaking out of my bedroom window at night to huff computer cleaner with boys and my mind is clean but the computer is filthy.

My mom is dragging me to the dry cleaners where the dry cleaner man has an abacus and an African gray parrot that says hello in a voice like a computer. I realize that my mom doesn't have to pick up dry cleaning at all, that she comes in just to pet the bird and feed it cashews through the bars of its cage. She's feeding the bird as I'm rolling my eyes and counting the seconds until I can watch makeup tutorials and drink 4Lokos and eat Tide Pods and compromise my mom's credit card information on Korean wholesale websites.

It's 102 degrees in Los Angeles and my mom is picking me up from the mall security office for shoplifting from Victoria's Secret. She is furious in the car like, "why do you need a rhinestone Bombshell anyway?" and I can't explain so we sit in silence in the Honda Civic listening to NPR which is playing *the sounds of Navajo Nation*. What I can't say is that I saw Lacey McKelvy changing for PE and she has the most insane rack I've seen on a seventh grader and I need a rhinestone Bombshell because when Lacey McKelvy saw me changing for PE she scoffed and there isn't a sound in Navajo Nation loud enough to drown out her scoff and the torque of her massive tits as we play capture the flag.

I'm lying on the bathroom floor after cutting my labia with safety scissors while trying to trim my pubic hair. My mom takes me to urgent care and totally loses it like, "what were you thinking, kid? It's not your fucking bangs," as she paces back and forth and tells me she was in labor for fifteen hours, "Do you know what that did to my vagina? It was like Vietnam down there." I tell her that Lacey McKelvy has enormous tits and I have nothing but a misdemeanor and a deviated labia and she looks at me as if through thick glass, squinting to see clearly but can't.

I take edibles with Hannah and ride the bus from the valley to Santa Monica which takes forever and by the time I get there I'm so high I can't navigate the boardwalk or my Motorola Razr to call for help and end up in a Bubba Gump Shrimp gazing into the lobster tank wondering how I could free all of the lobsters without the hostess noticing when suddenly Hannah's mom is picking us up because she's a cool mom who picks us up in Santa Monica and lets us sleep over and doesn't tell the uncool parents we were high and the boys call her a MILF and she even lets Hannah drive before she has her permit, not just in a parking lot but on the freeway and my mom is feeding cashews to the bird while Hannah is driving on the 405 and I'm so hungry I could eat a lobster. I'm thinking about the financial crisis and the profound depths of the universe while Hannah's mom is telling me about Heaven's Gate and the car is moving so fast and my heart is beating so fast it's like I'm on level:EXPERT but there isn't a bar to lean back on.

I'm twenty- four and everyone on Instagram has been sexually assaulted and I'm allowed to roll my skirt up as short as I want now because of #metoo and because there is no God and Trump's railing Adderall and Lauren Myracle died of cervical cancer and Dante went to jail for vehicular manslaughter and Lacey McKelvy is on OnlyFans and Mr. Gayworth adopted a beautiful baby girl and the dry cleaner man was deported. My mom mourns the bird and secretly cries for it at night and I wonder what happened to all of the simulated animals, if the Neopets starved to death. My mom's parents were immigrants from Ireland who lived through famine and witnessed civil war and car bombings and revolution and came to America with only $36 in their communal pockets and I lived through a moderate recession and monitor my caloric intake and the revolution was an arcade game and I can spend $36 on drinks at Good Luck Bar in a night easily. But the difference is that they were nothing. The difference is that I'm a Lutheran and an American and a hostage, perennially updating like a smartphone, barreling forward into the profound depths of the universe.

Earth Angel

ANIKA'S LITTLE BROTHER IS ON THE COUCH and watching Frozen 5 in Arabic. He tells her that Helen Keller was gay. There's new evidence. She nods. She asks if he's up for a walk. They used to walk every day before Dominic incurred several injuries to his tibia from the skateboarding incident. But he's probably fine now. Milking it, Anika thinks. She walks with Dominic limping several feet behind her. They stroll through the canyon until they crest the hill and look out over the city with ownership.

"Los Angeles is a fortress city," they say.

"Horribly disparate wealth distribution."

"Partisan officials. Draconian law enforcement."

"Built on oppression," Anika says, squeezing lemon into her hair because it's summer and the citrus gives her highlights.

"Osama Bin Laden was gay," says Dominic and Anika gives him a look meant to convey amusement with the younger generation. While Anika feels that she has plateaued culturally, her brother is perennially upgrading like a smartphone. He takes 60 milligrams of Adderall per day and speaks five languages. He's fatally allergic to shellfish and dairy and tree nuts and the sun's ultraviolet rays. He will grow up to be beautiful like Anika and gay like Osama Bin Laden.

They pass a hideous house.

"That house is hideous," says Dominic.

"That's the CEO's house," says Anika.

They tilt their heads at the house. It looks like a Soviet tenement building, lacking charm or empathy or landscaping. No discernible entrances or exits. Nowhere to welcome girl scouts or trick-or-treaters. It doesn't have clotheslines or a wrap-around porch or wind chimes or decals to keep birds from flying into the windows. It doesn't have windows. It has a "shot on sight" vibe, at stark odds with the rest of the cottagey properties that exude mirth and reverence for a simpler time. The canyon residents attend drum circles and contribute to community libraries. They know their rising signs and shop at farmer's markets and their unvaccinated children are visual learners.

The canyon looks like this:

And the CEO's house looks like this:

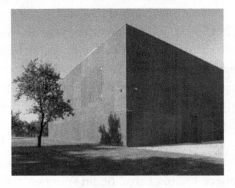

"Do you think he's in there?" asks Dominic.

"I've never seen anyone come in or out," says Anika.

Dominic flips off one of the cameras protruding from the CEO's house.

"I'm going to call the city," Anika continues. "We must have some architectural consistency laws or something."

Dominic hits his electronic cigarette which is flavored peaches and cream. Anika takes a pack of regular cigarettes out of the band of her leggings. She smokes three back-to-back Marlboro lights, depositing the butts in one of the canyon's many eco-blue recycling bins. They walk back to their house. Their parents are in Europe for the month. The house was bequeathed to the parents as a wedding present by their paternal grandmother who owns a foundry that manufactures steel for missiles. Their house is adequately bucolic, vine-swathed, paint chipping adorably off the little gate.

The AirMasterPro emits the smell of Rising Sourdough into the living room. Anika has a contract with AirMaster that she cannot dissolve. She clicked a box during her free trial that seems to have indentured her to the company, charging her $49.99 a month for the rest of her life. Every Wednesday she receives a shipment of scented pods from their extensive aroma catalog to feed the AirMaster. Lately they've been sending Anika Rising Sourdough so she can enjoy the olfactory sensation of bread while continuing to monitor her caloric consumption. But there's no limit to what you can smell: Christmas at Grandma's, Monday Night Football, Sweet Morning Dew, Shabbot Dinner, Craft Brewery, Factory Farm, Berlin Warehouse, Electrical Storm, Man-Made Lake, Hospital Cafeteria, Pacific Rim Wet Market... Anika has tried calling, emailing, canceling her credit cards. She was ready to throw in the towel until she learned that the CEO of the parent company, Nosi, built the hideous house right up the street.

The AirMaster's pods are extremely lethal when consumed, like pleasant-smelling cyanide tablets. There are rampant mass suicides and protests and a litany of lawsuits against Nosi. Those who ate the pods and survived later developed grotesque ailments like flesh-eating rashes and fevers and late-onset Schizophrenia and the longest-recorded nosebleed in history. Anika assumes the CEO built the bunker to protect against the process servers, angry mobs and hitmen who, like Anika, try to reach him daily. But perhaps, she thinks, he just wanted to create an eyesore to mess with yet another one of Anika's senses.

Anika's phone rings, and her voice dances up an octave as she answers. It's her boyfriend Jake Willner. Jake Willner is a regular on a popular sitcom called *Ghosted* about five twenty-somethings who move into a haunted loft in Portland. It's available on most streaming services. Jake Willner subjects Anika to frequent and primal psychological tortures. Sometimes he tosses the scent pods to the squirrels in her front yard and makes her watch as they eat them, their little bodies writhing and contorting until they slowly shut down. Anika tries not to read too much into this.

Jake Willner makes plans to have dinner with Anika then resumes watching accounts from Holocaust survivors. He looks up animals being slaughtered, cruel and inhumane conditions, abused dogs. He googles Bestgore and watches ISIS beheadings. He looks up incest porn. He takes a safety pin and pricks his arm several times. He holds a lighter to the tip of his penis, which hurts, but not in the way he wants. He imagines Anika being held down and gang-raped by a band of attractive burglars. He imagines her terminally ill, her body riddled with fast-growing cancers, lying in a hospital bed, holding his hand, saying she loves him and will wait for him in the ether. Nothing. It's the fault of women, he thinks. Women cornered the market on pain—labor, heartbreak, etc.—leaving nothing left for him.

Anika picks up Jake Willner for dinner. She tells him she's made reservations. Jake Willner says he doesn't feel like going to dinner, he feels like going to her parents house to fuck. Anika tells Jake Willner that they can't go to her parent's house to fuck and he asks why and she says because Dominic is there and he asks why and she says because he's a fourteen-year-old with an injured tibia from the skateboarding incident and where else would he be? Anika suggests that they return to his house, the house he alone owns at the age of twenty-five, after dinner for which she's already made a reservation. This suggestion fills Jake Willner with rage. He asks Anika to drop him off.

"I thought we were going out."

"I don't feel like it anymore."

Anika pulls the car over to the side of the road. There are billboards for AIDS and strip clubs and small defense lawyers above them.

"This isn't where I live," says Jake Willner.

"I'm not your driver," says Anika.

They sit in silence. Jake Willner imagines scraping out Anika's tongue with a soldering iron. There's an ad on the bus stop across from them for a skincare line featuring a well-known model.

"She's so pretty," says Jake Willner. "Perfect body."

"She doesn't have arms or legs," says Anika.

"You're just jealous of her," says Jake Willner.

"She's literally a torso," says Anika.

They stare at the model in fluorescent light hocking face cream. She stares back. Anika thinks how beautiful she is, how she really deserves to be a model and didn't deserve that quadruple amputation. Unless it was a career move in which case she gets it. It's hard being a woman in the workforce.

"Come on, Jake. What do you want?" Anika asks.

Jake Willner considers the question. Tonight he wants to punish Anika, but not so much that she'll leave him, just to test her limits. In general, he wants Anika to be lithe and chic and upbeat despite his despotism. He wants her to audit her weight when she's alone but not appear to watch what she eats when they go out. He doesn't want to know about the intricacies of her beauty routine. He's not the type of guy whose thoughts and desires are dictated by feminist rhetoric. He wants Anika hairless like a little girl but strong and opinionated like a woman. He wants to know that he comes before her career and wants her to know that she doesn't come before his. He wants her to understand that when they break up he'll find someone skinnier and chicer and better in bed and he wants her to question what she could have done differently, to understand that it was ultimately her shortcomings that drove him away. And he wants her to feel inclined to keep quiet so that her accounts of their relationship don't later damage his public image.

"I want to go home," says Jake Willner.

"I don't understand."

A couple breezes by on an electric scooter. Anika stares out the window. Jake Willner stares back from one of the billboards outside. *Ghosted* Season 7. *Who will be giving up the ghost?* Anika starts her car and drives Jake Willner home.

"I love you. I'm just feeling off tonight," says Jake Willner.

"Okay. Whatever," says Anika.

"What does whatever mean?"

"Whatever means whatever."

"It sounds like you're tacitly implying that I don't love you," says Jake Willner. "I'm lucky to have you. You're my rock. My earth angel. You hang the moon for me. I'd walk through hot coals for you."

"I just wanted to have dinner."

"I'll call you tomorrow."

"Okay," says Anika.

*

Anika drives back to the canyon and walks through the streets, which are now lit with old-fashioned lanterns, LED lights burning instead of Kerosene or whale oil or whatever—she doesn't know. The CCTV cameras on the streetlights are disguised inside birdhouses. The cool night air is thick with 5Gs. She walks until she crests the hill and looks out over the city with ownership.

She passes by the CEO's house. It looks abject in the dark. A prison. One of the metal panels opens and a car starts to pull in. Anika is surprised by the house's activity. She's used to it sitting dormant and stoic in the face of riots, protesters launching scent pods like tomatoes against its walls.

"Hey!" Anika yells at the driver.

The car stops. She approaches a tinted window. She doesn't recognize the brand of car but assumes that the doors open upward like bird's wings. Assumes that there aren't any fuzzy dice on the mirror. The window rolls down a crack.

"So you're my stalker," says the CEO.

"Hardly," says Anika.

The CEO slips her a piece of paper through the window. It's a note embossed with her initials on Hello Kitty stationery, one of many she'd written that week: *How dare you build a house like this in my idyllic neighborhood! PS Your company SUCKS and so do you :(. Love, Anika.*

"You left this outside my house, yes?" asks the CEO.

"You don't have a mailbox," says Anika.

"It's nicer than a lot of my other mail, I'll give you that. By the way, I have all my zoning permits. There aren't any architectural consistency laws here," says the CEO, rolling the window back up.

"Where are you going!"

"If I wanted to get accosted by crazy women, I would have stayed on Long Island."

"I just want to talk," says Anika.

"There is a 'feedback' section on my website," says the CEO.

"Can't I come inside?" asks Anika. "It's freezing."

"It's summer," says the CEO. The passenger door opens upwards like a bird's wing.

Anika knows that Jake Willner can see her movement. She's virtually accounted for at all times. She's a blue dot on a map. He's probably tracking her right now, waiting for her blue dot to land obediently back on her home coordinate for the evening so he can digitally tuck her in. She turns off her phone.

Anika is disappointed by the inside of the CEO's house. She expected aggressively uncomfortable furniture, exotic pets, taxidermied Angora rabbits, maybe a tropical fish tank or a free-roaming anaconda, metal sculptures twisted to resemble balloon animals. But it's normal, even a little tacky she thinks, sporting an unpleasant mixture of brown and black chairs. A Scarface poster. She notes a flannel beanbag chair with dark stains. There is one long window overlooking the city.

"I bet they don't have views like that on Long Island," says Anika.

"No, they don't have views of Los Angeles on Long Island," says the CEO.

"Do you have anything to drink?" asks Anika.

The CEO circumvents a marble kitchen island to the refrigerator and opens it. There's nothing inside but sparkling water and some baby bottles labeled breast milk.

"Oh, are you going to murder me?" Anika asks.

"They're my sister-in-law's. She and my brother are staying with me." The CEO gestures into the depths of the house. "She nurses all the time. It's pretty weird."

"Nursing isn't weird," says Anika.

"It's weird because her kid is like twelve."

She nods. "That is weird."

"I'm too high-profile to murder you anyway," says the CEO.

"If I had twenty dollars for every time I've heard that," says Anika.

"It's funny how that phrase changes as currency inflates," says the CEO.

"I guess. Not *ha ha* funny."

"So I'm not the only high-profile person in your life?"

"My boyfriend. He's on that show *Ghosted*."

"Mazel."

"You are kind of a murderer though," says Anika. "I mean, people are literally dying at your hand."

"The pods really aren't for consumption. It says so on the label," says the CEO

"You're killing the environment too," says Anika. "They aren't recyclable."

"True, but do you know that 30% of our proceeds go directly to saving the children?"

"Which children?"

"I don't know."

"Why did you build a house like this here?" asks Anika.

"I'm trying to avoid assassination before my 40th birthday. Anyway. There isn't a property here under four million. Why should I pretend to be living in a hippie commune?"

Anika thinks about the cameras. The Teslas with *Coexist* bumper stickers. It's a shabby-chic surveillance state. She's Mr. Rogers in Foucault's Panopticon. She sits down on the beanbag.

"I'm not sharing muffins with my neighbors like it's Burning Man when I make...well it's gauche to specify but suffice to say I can buy my own muffins," continues the CEO.

Anika turns on her phone to find eighty-seven texts from Jake Willner. She turns it back off.

"Can I smoke in here?"

"No."

"My boyfriend is upset with me," she says.

"The high-profile boyfriend?"

"Yes."

"That's a shame."

Anika tells the CEO about Jake Willner. His famous parents, a supermodel mother and movie star father, the product of what tabloids label a very unhealthy environment for a child. The parents just surfaced from a lengthy and public divorce and now his dad is in Denmark filming the third in a blockbuster series he stars in about Vikings. She talks about Jake Willner's charisma and how lucky she feels to be privy to his rare moments of vulnerability. How it endears him to her when he reads her texts while she's sleeping or in the shower because she knows he cares. How their volatile fighting always teeters on violence but never escalates, not while angry anyway. A few times during sex which she pretends to enjoy. How she thrives under his oppressive control, appreciates the regimentation and thinks his pendulous mood swings keep things interesting. How she hates to pick the dead squirrels off her lawn but how she loves to feel the looks of envy when she's on his arm at a party. Those looks alone could justify the rest.

"Your boyfriend's TV show is poorly written and it sounds like he's a psychopath," says the CEO.

"Then I think that I might be a psychopath, too," says Anika.

"I'm not getting that. You're a strong, beautiful, upper-middle class woman in modern America."

"Exactly. I'm unassailable. I need to take responsibility for creating the conditions of my own suffering."

"Can I kiss you?" asks the CEO.

"I think it kind of ruins it when you ask."

"I'm just trying to be…"

"I know."

She allows the CEO to kiss her. He leans over her on the beanbag. It sighs under their collective weight. He paws at her tights which are shellacked onto her skin. She whispers something about his extended family being home, not wanting to wake his perverted nephew. He puts a finger to his lip then shimmies her tights down enough to put his head between her legs.

"You don't have a wife or something, right?" Anika asks.

"No, I don't have a wife or something," says the CEO

"I think your company is heinous," says Anika.

"Thank you for the feedback," says the CEO.

Post-coital and unpromoted, Anika tells the CEO about the skateboarding incident. About the car that pulled out of the driveway and hit Dominic, splintering his tibia and his skateboard into pieces, how the latter of which upset him exponentially more than the former. How the X-ray looked like cracks in a frozen pond. How the car peeled off and fled the scene but Dominic's friend live-streamed the whole thing and the live-stream went viral and the driver was caught by the police and how Dominic didn't want to press charges because he ultimately hates cops more than he hates people who commit vehicular manslaughter or something like that. How Anika had been so mad at Dominic and pleaded with him to press charges because this felt like a precious unfettered instance of right and wrong but Dominic refused so Anika went rogue and employed Jake Willner, who has a known penchant for brutality, to find the driver and beat him mercilessly in the Trader Joe's parking lot, breaking his nose and jaw, because then at least things were even, an eye for an eye, a nose and jaw for a tibia and a skateboard, and if the whole world is blind, she says, then maybe its other senses will be heightened.

"I saw your brother on my security cameras earlier. He was flipping me off," says the CEO. He plays with Anika's hair, an expression of familiarity only warranted by their previous sexual act.

"You know, I have a subscription to AirMaster. I've been trying to cancel it."

"I know."

"What do you mean you know?"

"I know. I looked at everyone's files when I moved here."

"You know who I am?" asks Anika.

"I know your age and gender and address and that you smoke Marlboro Lights and like the smell of Rising Sourdough. I know you've endeavored to cancel your subscription several times. The AirMaster is recording and collecting data 24/7. Don't berate me about privacy. "Nosi" functions on several levels."

"Why do you need to know that stuff about me?"

"So we can draw informed conclusions about the consumer. Knowing your age, gender, and socio-economic standing tells us a lot about what you might want to smell."

"Wait, this is so f*cked up," Anika says with an asterisk, swallowing the "u."

"Scent is the bedrock of our psyche. Did you know that smell is the sense most closely associated with memory?" the CEO asks Anika. She does know. It says so on the AirMaster box. It's in the masthead on the website.

"I don't drink myself, but do you know what my favorite scent pod is?" the CEO asks. "Irish Whiskey. And do you know why? It's what my priest smelled like on Long Island. That's some sick shit. See what I'm saying? There's a reason my company grossed more than competitors like HeavenScent in its first 6 months. We personalize the experience. We're more than just an air freshener—I take offense to that term by the way—I'm selling nostalgia. Each pod is like a crystal ball."

"There are protests every day against your company," says Anika. She's seen them on the news. Crowds holding signs reading *Smell No Evil* or *Big Brother is Smelling* or *AirMaster and Commander* or *Don't be a Pod Person* or *Stop and Smell the Corporate Corruption.*

"That's nothing but theater. The people protesting outside my office don't really care about the environment or our testing on Labradoodles or the Serbian workers in the AirMaster factories breathing in monoxide and fiberglass. It's a production, just like your houses here masquerading as modest prairie homes as if they didn't cost more than most Americans will make in a lifetime. See how I've brought our conversation full circle? What? What is it?" The CEO looks at Anika. "You have this revelatory look on your face."

"I'm just realizing that…I have the worst taste in men," Anika says. These men are bullsh*t, she thinks. She doesn't need to listen to this. She's unassailable. She's a strong, beautiful, upper-middle class woman in modern America. An earth angel.

"I have to go," she says, clutching her Hello Kitty note.

"I wish you wouldn't," says the CEO. "You're very pretty and I'm enjoying our discourse."

"Please cancel my subscription and remove me from the Nosi email notifications."

The night outside is perforated by the fake lanterns. The first thing Anika registers as she steps onto the lawn is that the grass smells like sweet morning dew. Not an olfactory simulacrum. She turns back and flips off the CEO's security cameras. Her voicemail is full when she turns on her phone. She reads through a spectrum of texts from Jake Willner, threatening, then bargaining, then finally pleading her to answer. *Sorry, my phone died,* she responds. *Dinner tomorrow?* She walks home. Inside Dominic is awake, high on Adderall and making waffles without eggs or flour or milk or water.

Beauty Queen

THAT SUMMER GOD SPOKE to my little sister. He told her to win the Teen Miss Florida pageant. "Are you sure that's what He said?" I asked. I was drinking a lot back then and often misinterpreted the Lord's instructions. She was more or less certain.

Kids from our neighborhood were not in the business of winning beauty pageants. That's why she needed to break her legs. Or just one leg. One leg would do. The pageant circuit took pity on the injured—little girls on crutches who'd fallen from their horses. It pulled at their heartstrings. Get back in that saddle, etc.

So we took a sledgehammer from dad's tool shed. I expressed my reservations. About pageants in general. She said, "what's so wrong with commending great beauty?"

I said, "what's in it for me?" She considered. "You could write a story about it."

We went out to the backyard and sat on the rusted swing set. Looking at her posture as she sat—an imaginary encyclopedia balanced on her head—I thought she really could win. Perhaps even without being maimed. Why endure the suffering? "That's what's most beautiful of all," she said. Mustn't one know great suffering to understand great beauty? She was fourteen. There were wisps of fine hair on her knees.

As we stepped out onto the wet grass I told her we could still call the whole thing off. She said *please sissy* and the child looking back at me was Miss Florida. I could see it; sashes and sausage curls and world peace but moreover I could see that God was speaking through her. I was drinking a lot back then. She sat down in the grass and spread her legs apart making one point of a star. She closed her eyes and clasped her hands together in prayer. I raised the sledgehammer above my head.

Sponge Cake

Your mom is birdwatching, and you're thinking about rapists. She points out a woodpecker or something. She used to be a big name in publishing. Now she's retired. Now she makes sponge cake and points out woodpeckers. The walls are painted eggshell, so she's walking on eggshells as she's climbing the walls. She has the best landscaper in Connecticut. You wonder if your mom has a rapist. She'd have the best rapist in Connecticut. Her trees are so lush that they're top-heavy. Their trunks buckle under the weight of their foliage. *It's like they're suicidal,* says your mom. The best landscaper in Connecticut bolsters them with structural reinforcements.

Your mom asks if you slept on the flight here, and you tell her you don't sleep. You try to shower, but your mom's faucet is in French. It says "chaud" and "froid." It's too froid. It isn't froid enough. You think your mom could use a visit to Froid. She asks where your rapist is now, and you say he's in your pocket.

Your rapist is on Instagram, hanging out with everyone. Everyone is like, "so-and-so invited him." He used to be a big name in raping. Now he's retired. Now he hangs out with so-and-so, and "this must have been some fluke thing because he's a really nice guy if you get to know him," everyone tells you. The trees are suicidal, and it doesn't matter what language the shower is in, you never feel clean anyway.

You have trouble breathing at night. Your mom asks where your rapist is now, and you say he's in your lungs. You go for a walk on eggshells. Your mom's landscaper is the best in Connecticut. He waves you over to see where the trees are buckling. He tells you he got into the country in a shipping crate so small he had to dislocate his shoulder to fit inside. You tell him your rapist is on Instagram, hanging out with everyone. He says sometimes life throws a lot at you.

Your mom has a hybrid dog. You scratch its belly and pick up its shit. Once it dislocated your mom's shoulder by pulling too hard on the leash. She could have fit in a shipping crate. The dog cocks its head at you. It tells you that it used to be a person, a person who threw a quarter in a well during a lightning storm and woke up in the body of a hybrid dog in Connecticut. Some fluke thing. You're like, "why are you telling me this?" He says, "sometimes life throws a lot at you." You ask what it's like being a dog, and he says, "it has its days."

Your mom is making sponge cake, and you're thinking about rapists. Yours is a really nice guy if you get to know him. Your mom used to work in Paris. Now it's only Paris in her shower. Now she's buckling but bolstered with structural reinforcements. Now she's blanching the basil and deboning the branzino, and she's mastered the sponge cake which is very moist. "Don't pathologize the sponge cake," says your mom. "Eat up. Life is hard but not as hard as a stale sponge cake." She makes extra for the dog and the landscaper.

○

Mark's Turtles

~~~~~~~~~~~~~~~~~~~~~~~~~~~~~~~~~~~~~

I WAS IN A PINAFORE AND KNEE-HIGH SOCKS leaning against Mark's Chevy Malibu. Mark took photos of us in his backyard in Hollywood. Mark was like thirty-five I guessed. All adults were thirty-five. My friend Sophia told me to puff my lips out more. I had just gotten my braces off.

"No, like this," said Sophia.

"Yeah, like that," said Mark.

Mark knelt to compensate for our height difference.

"Great outfit," said Mark.

"Thanks," I said. I was in my school uniform.

I changed into my next outfit under my current outfit the way Sophia taught me. Mark gave me some sunglasses that weren't for the sun. Mark told me to peer over them.

"Like Lolita," said Mark.

"Don't smile so much," said Mark.

All of Mark's directions were counterintuitive. Don't smile and, if you do, smile with your eyes. Smile with your body. My body didn't smile. It played AYSO soccer. The only instruction I'd previously been given from someone behind a camera was: say *cheese*. Sophia told me to relax my jaw like I'd taken a Benadryl. She said to stop saying cheese. She said to think about photos of dust bowl families in our history class. Somber and malnourished. Think about famine when you pose. Think about the genocide. Model like you're being persecuted for your religion. You're Jesus stapled to the cross. I pushed my body against the car and frowned like Jesus.

"You're getting better," said Sophia.

"Who's Lolita?" I asked.

Mark was an amateur photographer that hung out with teenagers. He went to an all-ages nightclub in Hollywood every Wednesday. That's where I first met him. I was there with my older brother who had gotten out of jail a few months earlier. He was in jail for accidentally smothering his girlfriend during sex. We were there with my brother's new girlfriend who was embarrassing me to death. She squatted to pee in the alley outside and I watched it puddle around her heels. She hiked up her underwear and said to my brother, "your little sister was watching me piss. She gay or something?" and she lit a menthol cigarette which meant she'd never go to outer space.

I wore my brother's t-shirt as a dress which featured a band I'd never heard of and played Brick Breaker on my Blackberry in the corner. I was trying to beat my high score. Mark mistook me trying to beat my high score as an abject aloofness that had sexual purchase in the early 2000s. I overheard him ranting at these anorexic girls about steel beams and research chemicals and about Obama orchestrating drone strikes and perpetuating foreign wars and then he pointed to me and said, "this girl gets it." Mark thought I didn't care about anything. But I did care, deeply, about beating my high score in Brick Breaker. "You like [BAND]?" he asked me. I looked down at my shirt and said, "yeah" and he said, "fuck yeah." I stopped paying attention to my game and the little ball went cascading into the abyss. Mark asked if I saw [BAND] play at [VENUE] last year. I thought about what I was doing last year. I was getting my ears pierced at Claire's. I was horseback riding at Lutheran summer camp. An older girl was teaching me how to use a tampon. I wasn't seeing [BAND] play at [VENUE]. I said, "yeah" and he said, "fuck yeah!" Then he said, "could I take your picture sometime?" I said he could take my picture any old time and gave him my AOL email. Then my brother's girlfriend found me and said, "there you are" and gave Mark a weird look and drove us to Arby's because my brother was too fucked up to drive and I wouldn't have my license for another four years.

Mark reached out to my AOL email about the modeling. He asked me to come to his house after school. I asked if I could bring my friend Sophia because she was beautiful. He asked for a photo of her like this: *send pix :p*. I sent him Sophia's yearbook picture. All of the other kids were smiling in their yearbook pictures. Sophia was scowling. She looked perfectly miserable. Like she'd never been told to say *cheese*. Say *divorce*. Say *leprosy*. Say *ethnic cleansing*. Sophia's photo stood out on the glossy paper. One of these is not like the others. She transcended the watermark across her face. Mark said, "oh, fuck yeah!" He gave me directions to his house in Hollywood which I put into Mapquest and printed out. I told my Youth Government group that I wouldn't make our meeting. I told my mom I was seeing a movie. I torrented every album by [BAND].

We started going to Mark's every couple of weeks. He made us cocktails that were two parts vodka, one part blue Kool-aid. His house was filled with clothes. Pants and shirts and shoes organized respectively into piles like the Holocaust Museum. He had a tank of neglected turtles. Algae obscured their 360 view of Mark's bungalow. Sometimes he'd pour the remainder of his drink into their tank and the turtles would scurry out of the neon blue water onto their rotting log. He said it seeped into their skin and got them drunk.

Sophia was in her bra on Mark's living room floor. Mark was standing above Sophia who was modeling denim shorts but the focal point of the image wasn't so much the shorts as it was her neon blue tongue which she stuck out at the camera. He kept saying like, "this is great" and "one more for me." I was plastered to the sofa. One of these is not like the other. Sophia and I exchanged looks and she rolled her eyes like *grow up already* and so I grew up and joined her on the floor beneath Mark.

He told Sophia to kiss me. My first kiss had been the previous spring during a fire safety assembly with a Canadian eighth-grader called Jake Willner. His shiny forehead was stretched taut like a canvas showcasing several large and yellowing pimples. Sophia didn't kiss like Jake Willner. Sophia was beautiful. Sophia had milky skin and pouty lips. Sophia didn't say *cheese*. Sophia looked like an angel on Mark's shag carpet in the fluorescent glow of a wall sign that said *GIRLS! GIRLS! GIRLS!* Mark snapped the camera. Sophia and I rolled around on the ground. Our bodies picking up debris from the rug. The turtles swam helplessly through the two parts vodka. They scrawled *help us* on the murky tank walls. I rolled over a shard of glass and cut my arm. Sophia lapped at the blood with her tongue. Mark took pictures from above like, "this is great. This is awesome." I kept my eyes locked with the turtles.

> *This is great. This is awesome.*
> *Isn't this wonderful? Aren't you happy to be here?*
> *Look at this world I made for you.*
> *I said let there be light for you.*
> *I harnessed fire and parted seas and scoured deserts for you.*
> *I invented the wheel for you and you can't even drive.*
> *Tell me you're sorry.*
> *Frown like Jesus.*
> *Pose on my sim card.*
> *Wash my feet with your hair.*
> *Let me be your shepherd.*
> *Let me suckle your nectar and discard your husk.*
> *Let me create you in my image.*
> *This is great, one more for me.*

Mark's patio looked like a cartoon depiction of a junkyard. Sophia and I sat outside on the disemboweled backseat of a car. I was reading Animal Farm for school.

Mark looked at the book and said, "that book's a trip" and I said, "it's kind of bullshit honestly" and Sophia shot me a look like *don't disparage Animal Farm in front of the cool photographer.* Then I asked if I could have a bandage for the cut on my arm and they both looked at me like I was being voted off the island. Like I was first to die in the horror movie. They understood that I had never been cool. I had just been playing Brick Breaker.

Sophia stayed at Mark's house. She told me it was okay. He gave me some stickers with his name on them as I was leaving which ended up on all my binders. I walked three blocks down the street to Fairfax where my mom thought I'd been seeing a movie. My mom was wearing her scrubs when she picked me up and looked like she hadn't slept in a million years because she hadn't. She was working the night shift at a county hospital. I was quiet in her passenger seat and she leaned over and touched my forehead and said something like, "I'm so proud of you, Madeline. I know I've been working a ton but you're a good kid and I love you to pieces and you hang the moon for me and all of this is for you." Or something like that. She said maybe she'd save up and by summer we could take a road trip, just me and her. Then she asked how the movie was and I recounted the plot I'd read on Google earlier.

TGIF

~~~~~~~~~~~~~~~~~~~~~~~

STEPH LINES THE WALLS OF HER OFFICE with Tibetan prayer flags that look like swastikas. She has Kanji tattoos saying 悪因悪果 that she's never bothered to translate. Steph is a citizen of the world. She buys makeup that hasn't been tested on animals. Her gel nails fly over the keyboard as she makes meeting after meeting. She's the best assistant they've ever had.

I'm the worst assistant they've ever had. I type zero words per minute. My Gmail never empties. It's a renewable resource, a digital hot spring. My inbox runneth over. I don't care if my makeup is tested on animals. I imagine lab rats with up to 36% lash volume.

Rachel from accounting has 6,000 unused vacation days and she'll never use them. She vacations to the break room. An app teaches her French. She has a tiny Eiffel Tower paperweight. It's Paris on the expense reports, on the loan forms, on the parking permits.

Bradford from marketing is falling in love with an ISIS recruiter online. They met in a singles chatroom. Sometimes she tells Bradford that to update the Koran is to deny its initial perfection. He's started calling us infidels. It's an HR nightmare. I feel happy for Bradford when I catch him gazing into the monitor as though into the eyes of a lover. I hope to meet that special someone someday.

Shara nurses in the lobby and the men go the long way to the kitchen to catch a glimpse, not of Shara's breasts, but of the child hanging off of them who is twelve. He's in varsity water polo. The breast milk gives him strength to play Fortnite.

I think about the black and white photo of the construction workers having lunch on the scaffolding. Those men aren't up there anymore. They're backend coders. They buy Bitcoin and pitch up their voices on Ableton. They're on my For You page because they're for me. We're the American workforce and our scaffolding is on Zoom.

The office is purgatory and I'm doing limbo in limbo. How low can I go? I wait for Bradford to start a caliphate and burn it all down. I clean the Mr. Coffee and watch the aquarium fish float through their fish castle.

Rachel says TGIF and we go out for drinks. Bradford

thanks Allah it's Friday. We cheers to our 401ks, our health insurance, our dental. We're a family: me, Steph, Rachel, Bradford, Shara, and the Mr. Coffee. It's happy hour and for that hour we're happy.

Little Dalmatia

I HEARD SOME GIRLS SAY THAT GOD was absent from our town. All the girls at the all-girls Catholic school had experienced something that fell under the nuance of rape. If a girl at the all-girls Catholic school experienced rape, they were to fill out paperwork in the counseling office and file it in the main office. When Gracie had sexual violence done to her by Jude Thomas from the all-boys Catholic school, she filled out paperwork in the counseling office and filed it in the main office. "Now what?" asked Gracie. "That's about it," we said. So Gracie started drugging Jude Thomas. She crushed up her birth control pills and mixed them into his protein powder before water polo. All semester Jude Thomas took birth control. Jude Thomas grew irritable and sensitive and sprouted breast buds and listened to Lana Del Rey. "Now he understands what it's like," said Gracie, "to be a girl." Gracie was sent away to a Swiss boarding school. Jude Thomas got a full ride to Penn State for water polo. This all happened in the absence of God.

I snuck a Croatian boy home with me. My dad caught us undressing in the pool house and chased the boy down the driveway with a hunting rifle. *Fucking Croom kid* he called after him. My dad couldn't run further. "If you touch her again, I'll put a hole in your head." He hurt his knee in the Navy. The knee had a plate in it that set off the metal detectors at airports.

San Pedro has the largest diaspora of Croatian immigrants in the country. Colloquially, that four miles of shoreline was called Little Dalmatia. We had pejorative terms for them; *Crooms*—referring to when Yugoslavia was part of greater Bosnia. But the slurs only betrayed a deep understanding of Slavic culture. The Croatians worked in the harbor and lived in row homes and used tap water tainted by runoff from the oil refinery. The longshoremen's wives packed them seafood pasta they'd eat between loading and unloading the cargo ships.

I lived a mile up the hill in Palos Verdes overlooking the harbor. *Verdes* is Spanish—the language the gardeners spoke—or green—the color they kept the lawns. All of the smog that settled over Little Dalmatia dissipated up the hill. We had a golf course and a tennis court and an equestrian center and a Catholic church and a Lutheran church and a Protestant church and an Episcopalian church and an Equinox. Our tap water was filtered.

I knew that God was absent from our town when the Reverend quit. There were rumors that the Reverend quit after Ben Sharlack from the all-boys Catholic school went to confession. The ladies who play Canasta in the back room saw Ben Sharlack leave a note in the confessional and the next day, the Reverend transferred to another parish.

I snuck out of my bedroom window and walked a mile down the hill to meet the Croatian boy. I apologized on behalf of my dad, and he shrugged like *these things happen* and rolled me a cigarette. His hands had grease on them from fixing his bike chain. We snuck into a shipping crate in the harbor, and I coaxed his hand under my uniform skirt. He asked me why, if I had so much money, did I look like a starving orphan? Outside we watched smoke plumes ripple off the oil refinery as giant machines distilled asphalt and petroleum.

A tenth-grade girl went missing after school. She never showed up to softball practice. The team waited and waited. She never showed up to cello or Shakespeare Club or Youth Government. The neighborhood held a vigil. There were stories that she'd been kidnapped by the Croatians and was being held for ransom. We waited for her finger to show up in her parents' mailbox. Still wearing her mood ring; milky pink and indigo swirls. Pink = scared. Indigo = hungry. All of our mood rings were indigo. We were all Chinese-gymnast-skinny. It turned out that the tenth-grade girl had run away with her dad's business partner. Her parents didn't get her finger in their mailbox. They got a postcard from Crete. Her fingers were all left intact, in fact, they had a French manicure.

A snooping Sunday School girl found Ben Sharlack's confession and posted it on Instagram. This is what it said:

Forgive me father for I have sinned. That's how you kick these things off, right? I cheated on the AP stats final. I stole a pack of gum from the Minimart. But what I most want to confess, Reverend, is that your son gives me head every Wednesday morning in the church parking lot. I'm pretty hard on him in school and for that I am sorry because every Wednesday morning while he's sucking me off and looking up at me with those big blue eyes I think about how much he means to me.

After my mom left, my dad bagged up her clothes and donated them to the Catholic church. He started dating the down-syndrome girl's mom. He paid for her to have her breasts done. I invited the down-syndrome girl to a sleepover but she declined. She said she didn't want to be my sister. She ignored me at mass while our parents held hands in the pew.

A Colombian exchange student transferred to our school. We invited her to a sleepover. At the sleepover the girls told secrets and we asked the Colombian girl to tell us a secret and she did. She told us that once she hit a hitchhiker while she was driving on a dark road in Colombia. It all happened so fast that she just kept driving and never told a soul until she came to America to attend our high school and told us at the sleepover. That was the best secret we'd heard in a while. We told her she'd be fine here because, for the most part, God was absent from our town. When the girls went to sleep I snuck back out to meet the Croatian boy whose hands were perennially slick with bike grease. I laid in his arms and told him about Gracie and Jude Thomas and the Colombian exchange student who'd committed vehicular manslaughter and the missing tenth-grader who wasn't missing at all.

I walked home early Wednesday morning through the church parking lot. Ben Sharlack was leaning against the wall with his hands in his pockets and looking into the distance.

"What are you waiting for?" I asked.

He shrugged like he didn't really know.

I ironed my skirt while my dad read the paper. I dabbed at the grease stains and he glanced up and said, "what's that from?" I said I must have sat in something at the horse stables and for a moment he knew. He knew I hadn't sat in anything at the horse stables. I could almost see him limping the mile down the hill to the harbor. I could see myself chasing after him in my bike shorts crying, "daddy no!" until he found the Croatian boy and I could see my dad shooting him in the head with the hunting rifle in Little Dalmatia while the longshoremen ate their pasta and the oil refinery distilled petroleum. But instead he just said, "be more careful. Those skirts are expensive."

Hollywood Tours

Al Friedman and his mentally-ill cousin painted a decommissioned school bus to say HOLLYWOOD TOURS. They charged tourists $10.00 or ¥1,186.24 or £7.64 and drove them on a 3.5-mile loop of the hills. The price was well under market rate for the industry, said Al. He spoke to the tourists through a headset. "Kurt Cobain used to live there," said Al, and so on. Al had been dishonorably discharged from the military. I don't know why. He started teaching English at a charter high school in the valley where he fell in love with an exchange student from Dubrovnik who broke his heart. Then he started doing Hollywood Tours. Al was my teacher when I met him. I called him Mr. Friedman then but now I call him Al.

"There isn't a moment I don't think about her," said Al.

"Think about who," I said.

"Katja," said Al.

I had to respect Al's passion for eleventh-grade literature. Year after year he was newly grief-stricken to find Gatsby dead in the pool. There'd be tears in his eyes. He was emotionally in tune. I don't know why I hung around Al after high school. I guess I thought he was going to do something great. Mostly because he was always saying he was going to do something great. When people called Al a loser he said just wait and see. When people called Al a pedophile he said the age of consent was different in Croatia. Al touched me with his resilience. "One day," he said, "you're going to turn on the news and say, *That's Al Friedman! He taught me English.*"

Every morning smelled like rotting Thai food in our neighborhood. The dumpsters baked with yesterday's pad kee mao. Our apartment was small. That stretch of Hollywood Boulevard was populated almost exclusively by members of the Thai diaspora. The Thai men loved my girlfriend. She wore sheer nightgowns to the laundromat and they tipped their newsboy caps to her, when they had them on. She liked their golden shrines piled with fruit offerings.

My girlfriend wrote storylines for video games. Her job was coming up with war crimes. Every day she thought of ways to desecrate the digital Middle East. In her nightgown she was a demolitions expert, a sniper, an instrument of torture. She paid our cheap rent by plotting air strikes.

I paid our rent by giving Hollywood Tours with Al and his cousin. Al wore his U.S. ARMY hat and khaki pants and Dockers. Sometimes we stood on the street holding a sign that read HOLLYWOOD TOURS $10.00 or ¥1,186.24 or £7.64. Sometimes a former student of Al's would recognize him and say, "Mr. Friedman?" and Al would say, "you must have me mistaken — " and they would say, "no, it's definitely you. Hey guys, look this guy taught me English. Damn, didn't you get fired for sleeping with an underaged — " and then Al's cousin would shoo them away and Al would pull his hat down over his eyes.

Al crossed himself when we drove past a church. He was brought up Catholic. He was God-fearing. He told me it never hurts to say a prayer. I asked Al when he prayed.

"Whenever I'm on my knees," said Al.

Al used his cousin's disability money to rent a warehouse in Chinatown. I spent evenings there while my girlfriend was droning maternity wards. Al said the warehouse was a condemned sweatshop. He said we could forgive its sinister history and give it new life. It didn't have air conditioning and the water ran brown. A feral cat wandered in and gave birth. Our friend Lucien moved in. He told us *the big one* was coming. We should all migrate inland. The parts of the city that weren't underwater would be on fire. He was buying land in Montana. Runaway high school girls moved in and slept on single mattresses like in an orphanage. They showed little interest in Al. He loved them. To him, they were each Katja.

"This is where they shot *Rush Hour*," Al told the girls.

"Okay," they said. "So what?"

"Sorry," said Al. "Force of habit."

A psychic moved into the warehouse for a couple of weeks. She told us who we had been in past lives. A macaw. A Turkish peasant. An oak tree. "This is your last life," the psychic told Al. He nodded as though she had confirmed something he already knew.

Al befriended the twin sisters. Their dad owned oil in Kuwait. He lived in the Hamptons and evaded taxes. The girls had come out West for the summer. They seemed delicate, like Fabergé eggs. Frail. Flat-chested. They didn't wear makeup. When it rained, which it rarely did, Al said the water pooled in their collarbones. It was all novelty to them: the warehouse, the school bus, the feral kittens. My girlfriend called them misery tourists. Their collective eyes lit up when they saw a rat returning from the dumpster.

The summer belonged to Al. In the warehouse, Al was not a loser. He was a landlord. He worked out daily. He did pull-ups on low-hanging pipes. He kept a miniature refrigerator stocked with unpasteurized milk that he drank from the carton. He said he was training for the L.A. Marathon. He would win and spend the prize money on an Alaskan cruise. He would be on the receiving end of a tour.

"You ever been up to Alaska?" he asked me.

"Never," I said.

"The light," said Al. "It's different up there."

The twins threw parties in Al's warehouse. Funded by oil. This was their first life. They wore ballet slippers. They wore dresses made of crinoline and chiffon that laced up their backs. In the latticed light of the warehouse, they were interchangeable. Nondescript angels of the Chinatown sweatshop.

While Al trained, his cousin put morbid Scandinavian pornography on an old, boxy television. His cousin didn't show much libidinal interest in the video. It played on repeat like a program in the background of a doctor's office. Al's uniform slowly changed. He shed the U.S. ARMY hat. He wore a partially unbuttoned Hawaiian shirt and open-toed sandals despite the broken glass that had accumulated on the floor. He let some kids paint a mural on the wall. It read **HOLLYWOOD TOURS** and Al welled up at the gesture. He was emotionally in tune. My girlfriend came to the warehouse one night. He hugged her hello and her body stiffened in his arms. She left quickly, she said, to avoid contracting dysentery.

The summer was ending. I closed our window to keep the smell of rancid noodles at bay. My girlfriend had her rangefinder focused on an enemy camp. She said I needed to stop hanging out with Al. I needed to stop giving Hollywood Tours. She said Al was a loser and a pedophile and I said that the age of consent was different in — and she said, "seriously, it's time." She said Al was on a perennial tour. But there was more out there for me. There was not more out there for the soldiers in her viewfinder. She pulled the trigger.

Al was benching 250. His arms bulged under his Hawaiian shirt. He grew irritable. He didn't check the mail and the warehouse lost power. Al's cousin's television went dark. Without the porn to validate its existence, the television became obsolete. Became a table. An ashtray. The warehouse reeked of spoiled milk. Al himself smelled like he was rotting internally. His eyes were glassy. His tours were decreasing in popularity. The bus amassed parking tickets. A patented tour company sent Al a cease-and-desist. My girlfriend said, "get a job, get a job, get a job."

I sat with Al and his cousin and eleven to fifteen tourists in the decommissioned school bus. "Keith Richards used to live there," said Al, and so on. I told Al that we needed to stop. I told Al that we were stuck on a loop. He said he knew we were on a loop — a 3.5-mile loop of the hills. I shook my head. I gave my resignation. He said he understood.

"You and me had a good run," I said.
"You and *I*," said Al.
"Sorry," said Al.
His cousin glared at me from the driver's seat.

I got a job in an office. I bought some nicer clothes. My health was insured, as were my teeth. I called my parents. My girlfriend was happy. Our combined salaries allowed us to move into a bigger place. We left fruit offerings outside the old apartment. As we drove away I said, "we used to live there."

Al gave up the lease to the warehouse. The twins checked into a charmless hotel by the water. Lucien moved to Montana. The runaway girls went home, went to college, became feminists, started podcasts. Al got a DUI and the tour bus was impounded. I went with him to pick it up and it was clear that he had been living inside it.

A sleeping bag. Empty milk cartons on the floor. Tin foil and translucent lighters which suggested drug use. Baggies of meth which suggested drug use. I paid the towing fee and Al told me he would pay me back when he won the L.A. Marathon. We didn't speak after that. I heard he was tutoring in English. I heard he was working at a Halloween Superstore. I heard he and his cousin were busking on the Venice Boardwalk. Then I heard nothing for a long time.

Our new neighborhood didn't smell like anything. I talked to my girlfriend's stomach. "Your mom drops napalm on civilians for a living," I told her stomach. We went to the market together. We avoided seed oils together. We went to a psychic in the valley who read the lines in our palms. Money, love and life. Her palm suggested motherhood. Mine vitamin deficiency. We drove home palm in palm down the 101.

I was on my knees making a mobile when my girlfriend said, "oh my god," to the news. I stopped making the mobile. The news said that the daughter of a wealthy oil tycoon had been kidnapped. Surveillance cameras caught her being hoisted into a makeshift sightseeing van. Her family found a note. She was being held for ransom: $1,000,000.00 or ¥118,607,000.00 or £761,235.00. Well under market rate as far as kidnappings go. The news asked that anyone with any information on her whereabouts report to the precinct immediately. The victim's twin, through teary eyes, pleaded for her sister's safe return.

"Oh my god," repeated my girlfriend.

I felt a wave of carsickness.

"What are you doing?" said my girlfriend.

Since I was already on my knees, I said a prayer. I said a
prayer for Mr. Friedman and his cousin and the beautiful,
young oligarch. I said a prayer for my girlfriend and her
stomach and Lucien and Katja. I thought about what it
must have been like, year after year, to find Gatsby dead
in the pool. "Oh my God," I repeated. Then I told my
girlfriend that I loved her and was lucky to have her. I
apologized for my shortcomings and told her I was going
to take her to Alaska where the light was different. She said
that that was a lovely sentiment but we needed to go down
to the precinct now.

"Have you seen this man?" said the news.

"That's Al Friedman," I said aloud. "He taught me
English."

My girlfriend's viewfinder was set on Al. I thought
about what it must have been like, year after year, to find
Gatsby dead in the pool.

I felt a wave of carsickness as we pulled out of the
driveway. We passed a man flipping a sign on the street
outside of a cell phone store. We turned on the radio for
updates on Al but there was only mariachi music. Stock
updates. Then static, static, static.

Fortune Teller

~~~~~~

"SEET, SEET," SAID THE PSYCHIC so the girl sat.
She gazed into the ball.

"Vat do you see?" asked the psychic.

The girl saw shag carpet. She saw the Ukrainian
woman's overgrown acrylics tapping the mildewed
tablecloth. She saw a concrete wall adorned with totems to
conflicting ideologies—prayer flags, a crucifix, a portrait
of Ganesh—and the reflection of the neon sign outside:
WHAT DOES Y UR FUTURE H LD? FORTUNE T
LLER $10.95.

"I don't see anything," said the girl.

"No, ees s'good. Look harder," said the psychic so the
girl looked harder at the ball, into the crystal stratus.

"I see myself," said the girl, squinting. "And I'm married
to a handsome man. He has a lucrative career in finance
and we have a child. A little girl. She's retained our best

features and will be a model."

"Vat else?" asked the psychic.

"We have a house," said the girl. "With lots of land yet in close proximity to the city. It has bay windows and a wrap-around porch and blue toile wallpaper and a smart speaker that sends us targeted advertisements for beautiful linens. We have a healthy relationship with capitalism. There are stables outside with two horses and a foal. We have an apartment in the city as well. It overlooks the park. It's in the best school district. We have an eco-friendly car. We travel in the summers to places with translucent waters. Our daughter gets to see the world. She speaks three languages."

"Vat else?" asked the psychic, hitting a vape pen. The girl leaned in closer to the ball.

"My husband is a good man," said the girl, "but it appears that once a month he binds me hand and foot and administers ritualistic punishments to my feet, abdomen, and inner thighs that consist of drizzling organic honey onto my skin and releasing malnourished fire ants which he otherwise keeps in a vial. We must attribute the subsequent welts to eczema and late-onset acne when friends and coworkers inquire. My husband thinks the ritual will bring us good fortune. He's not wrong so far."

"Vat else?" asked the psychic, filing a nail.

"My daughter attends the best private school in the city where the children harvest vegetables and play wood instruments. Unfortunately, she inherits her father's penchant for torture and executes the class hamster with a shiv she fastens out of popsicle sticks. The teacher sees the lack of remorse in her young eyes and wants to have her put away, sent to a facility for adolescent psychopaths run on government funding so my husband and I pull her out of school and leave town. Our eco-friendly car cannot travel long distances so we abandon it roadside and continue on foot. Our house in the country has been seized and foreclosed upon when it comes to light that my husband committed a litany of financial crimes to afford it and our many Caribbean and Polynesian recesses. So we head west. Due to rising sea levels and shifting plates, the coasts have become inhospitable and their only inhabitants are escaped convicts and political exiles living in abject poverty. Hollywood Boulevard is a third world country. The streets are buckled and the walk of fame is illegible. The gift shops were looted and the Chinese Theater burned. We sleep in the pews of a Catholic Church where the altar has been tagged with spray paint to read: *THERE IS NO GOD*. There's no electricity nor running water. We enroll our daughter in a local public school where there are no class pets to kill. The kids learn to operate firearms. My husband continues to chastise my feet, abdomen, and inner thighs, although there is no more honey since there are no more bees. They committed mass suicide. They abandoned their queen. So my husband makes do with water from the blackened Pacific."

"Vat else?" asked the psychic, stifling a yawn.

"Our daughter joins a satanic cult, shaves her head, starts a countercultural podcast. She marries a man like her father. Starvation and manual labor does wonders for my figure. I need no Peloton. I look like Emrata. We find an old newspaper and read about pedophilic government cabals. We read that Florida is underwater. We do the crossword and watch as the disintegrating ozone ripples like heat on pavement. Like television static." The girl looked up from the ball.

"Zat vill be $10.95," said the psychic.

Water Sports

THE ACTOR WANTED TO BE FAMOUS, but more than fame, the actor wanted to torture his girlfriend. He nudged her underwear with his toe—a wisp of fabric crumpled beyond recognition like a dehydrated jellyfish. He thought of stuffing it down his girlfriend's pretty throat, using her own garment against her. He thought of carving up her pretty skin with increasingly dull and unsterile instruments.

He fought this urge. One week, demanded his agent. One routine week without incident. He could not risk another blow to his precarious stardom. He was already on thin cultural ice after what he did to a statue of bell hooks. Plus his girlfriend was away, getting college credit for removing single-use plastic from the Atlantic Ocean.

The actor scrolled dual monitors for his name. The first AI-piloted heart transplant patient was recovering successfully. A new virus was spreading that only affected lesbians and immigrants. An album was released by a rapper who possessed the negative physical qualities of both genders. An aging literary critic was being chastised for the twenty-three-year-old company he kept. Ads for Coin.fession leaped over the screen; decentralize your sins, mint eternity. Excluded from yet another news cycle, the actor sank deeper into a state of fear. Fear that he would fall from social prominence as quickly as he had ascended. SOMETIMES IT'S GOOD TO LIVE IN FEAR, said an ad for unpasteurized milk.

He slowly dressed for that night's fête; a museum benefit that took place on the catamaran of a wealthy benefactor—the Basquiyacht quipped the invitation. He hated boats. He hated water generally unless he was holding his girlfriend under it.

The critic nursed a cigarette and watched the gentle pulse of the Greenpoint pier. He observed the cynosure of the moment glide onto the ship. Noah's social ark, he thought and filed the thought away for later use. The kids and their looks of *wow, I didn't expect to run into anyone while on this media-frequented cruise* amused the critic until it came time for him to board and he felt a pang of schoolyard fear. Fear he might be chided for his exploits with this or that model. Fear of being ridiculed for his senescence. His iconoclasm, obsolete profession, and oversized Dockers. Fear of being another fossil in the maritime Met. SOMETIMES IT'S GOOD TO LIVE IN FEAR said a billboard advertising tourism in Somalia.

The critic had been subsiding off royalties from his last essay, a palatable rumination on generational differences in the technological age, lauded for its exploration of politics and morality without the imperatives of capitalism. He thought about his next piece. What if Starbucks had been named after a different character in Moby Dick? He filed that thought away for later inspection.

His agent called as the critic plodded down the dock. "You don't make my job easy."

The girls that passed did not have the crepe paper skin of his female peers. Each debutante to flit by the critic was more radiant than the last, more youthful, more apt at employing the aesthetics of great famine. One—perhaps they'd met before, perhaps she'd enjoyed his rumination on generational differences—smiled at him, beckoning him onto the barge. His agent still:

"Did you hear me?"

"Say it again."

"I said it's funny that you write so much about time and yet are always late."

"I'm going to have to cancel our lunch. I'm getting on a boat."

"Please don't talk to anyone. Especially women."

The young writer waded through the congested ship, mentally comparing the swaying bodies to wind-blown cattails like the ones that grew in Colorado, her place of origin which a friend had disparagingly referred to as a "fly-over state" recently and in response the writer had laughed because being self-aware, she decided, was more important than being proud of one's heritage.

Breaking through, as it were, proved difficult for the young writer who had written little more than ad copy since arriving in the city. That said, her LIVING IN FEAR campaign, albeit soul-sucking had been quite lucrative. When her break did finally reveal itself, it was in the form of an aging literary critic whose corrugated skin the writer mentally compared to the hide of the cattle she tended back home.

Her friend assured the writer that the aging critic did not want to read her musings on rural Colorado. But the critic might like to sleep with her and she could perhaps benefit off the sexual reciprocity. "Lie about your age," advised her friend. The writer, age twenty-three, did not know in which direction she should lie. She spent an evening the week prior at the critic's favorite bar, hanging on his every word, laughing when appropriate and nodding sage-like when wisdom was bestowed. "I love how you explore politics and morality without the imperatives of capitalism," she had said in a breathy, suggestive tone. She had even picked up the bill because the critic had forgotten his wallet.

When arriving on the boat, the writer's friend lent her

a bottle of Korean hair oil that was "the best" but also "really flammable" with which the writer lathered her hair until it was flaxen and lustrous like, she compared mentally, the mane of her childhood Clydesdale. A photographer in a revealing Hawaiian shirt snapped her portrait confirming the efficacy of the oil. She looked out over the party, through the cargoed bodies, and into the breakwater waiting for the aging critic and the subsequent advancement of her literary career.

The photographer wanted one thing, and one thing only: multiple titties shoved in his mouth. He did not have a preference in size, shape or color. There was no quenching his libidinal thirst without fondling every fledgling model in downtown New York. Just today he had awoken with two girls he met the night prior, spent the morning sucking and palpating, performing his erotic mammograms. But he still was not satisfied and now, on the boat, it took every ounce of his discipline to mind the popular adage *eyes up here.*

Oh the innovations late-feminism made in women's clothing, or lack thereof, liberating the nipple, the freedom for which he had been a long-time advocate. He learned early on in his career—his heyday, the '90s—that if you wear a camera around your neck, girls will often expose themselves to you as an act of playful rebellion. And he could only hope that if breasts were flashed in the first act of the boat party, they would be mashed in his face by the third.

An hour off-shore and the glitterati were getting queasy. The girls steadied themselves on their dates, their pallor turning from white to green. As the sun began its descent and the ship circled the greenest girl of them all, Lady Liberty, the crowd fell into a state of collective seasickness. The photographer watched in revulsion as, one by one, the women began ejecting their meager dinners onto the bow, each inspiring the next, like nauseated dominos.

He was immune to the mal de mer because, before becoming a famed party paparazzo, he had served three years in the naval academy, once notably telling *Page Six* that it was "so clutch" to be in the Navy during a ground war. He had spent most of his active service playing Halo. Now chaos mounted. With vomit came slippage, followed by injury. Blood and bile. The city's finest were falling into their own foul messes. Clothing was removed and engaged tactically; tube top as tourniquet, etc. Utilitarian nudity. The photographer got his wish, against all odds, of seeing some cleavage.

He made his way to safety on the boat's lower deck, scraping the dregs of some congealed cocaine out of a glass vial. In his haste, the photographer bumped into a couple—a young girl draped coquettishly over an old man whom the photographer recognized from tabloids exposing the man for doing exactly this—spilling what appeared to be a bottle of Korean hair product. Startled, the old man dropped his lit cigarette into the puddling oil.

A beautiful young activist donning a yellow life preserver stabbed at the briny shell of Trash Island. She'd save this gentle planet yet, spreading the word of her benevolent God to even the most jaded and impenetrable of communities. She wandered off from her cohort of volunteers for a moment of solitary prayer. Oh Jesus, if only she could remove the plastic bags and six-pack ringlets from her relationship. It had become more volatile as of late during her boyfriend's social acclivity. Sometimes verging on violent. A light in his eyes, thought the activist, had been snuffed.

Tears filled the activist's eyes at the realization of her own helplessness. She knelt in a nest of disposable straws and wept. She could not be a hero to everyone—the ozone, the oceans, the inbred chickens—least of all herself, without making some difficult choices. "God, give me a sign," she pleaded, when out in the distance her miracle appeared. Her burning bush. The Lord incarnate: in the middle of the sea, a tiny fire sat on the horizon, appearing no bigger than the plume of a lighter.

○

Good Boy

~~~~~~~~~~~~~~~~~~~~~~~~~~~~~~~~~~~

THE DOG MURDERER COULDN'T HAVE
BEEN older than twenty-one. She had soft, pink skin and
a veil of Invisalign over her teeth, gapped like a Swiss
model. She looked like the star of a video I was fond of by
XXXploitedTeens.com. Maybe it was the same girl. This
could be common—I wouldn't know. There could be a
direct porn to veterinary vocational pipeline.

The dog had dog hemorrhoids. He had dog cancer. He
had a litany of ailments that made it hard to be a dog.
So my mom put a hit on him. She paid $600 to have the
dog murdered, cremated and returned in a dog urn. They
come to your home which I was told makes the execution
more civil. My mom and sister and I sat on the floor
petting Cashew until it was time and on the floor I thought
about two things: The first thing I thought about was how

incredibly attractive the dog murderer was. Even had she
not made amateur sex videos, her scrubs betrayed enough
of her body that I could tell it was the stuff of male fantasy.
I forgot the second thing I thought about.

She sat down with us on the floor. *Blind?* she whispered.
I looked into Cashew's milky, cataracted eyes that had
overseen so much of my childhood, now smudged camera
lenses. *Mostly, yeah* my mom said. The dog murderer
nodded sage-like and rifled through her duffle bag. I
thought she might pull out a handgun. She didn't. She was
very professional.

As the sedative was administered and Cashew relaxed
over our communal laps, my sister started to cry. Then my
mom started to cry. I couldn't take my eyes off the dog
murderer's tits. Only made more arousing that they were
obscured by so much polyester. I wondered what she did on
weekends. When she wasn't euthanizing family pets. She
probably laughed and drank and danced—read in a nook
by the window or something. Cashew watched her with
his murky, all-knowing gaze. His angel of death. Perhaps
the company orchestrated it this way. They wanted the last
thing the animals saw to be beautiful.

My mom took my hand as the needle juiced up and
the final shot was prepared. The dog murderer cooed
good boy to Cashew and blood flowed to my crotch. The
smell of synthetic chemicals and medical regalia was
an aphrodisiac. I shut my eyes and tried to think about
something horrible. I thought about putting my dog to
sleep while my mom held my hand. But with my eyes

closed all I saw was XXXploitedTeens. POV: the dog murderer on her knees. I was scratching behind her ear. She was kicking her leg. Then my sister yelled *ohmygod! Do you have a boner right now?!* I opened my eyes. My family balked. Cashew's killer regarded me like a sick Labrador.

I excused myself and sequestered in the bathroom, my grass-stained lacrosse jersey flung over the shower rod. Splashing water on my face didn't help curb the desire. It was a waterfall. A locker room shower. A hot summer rain. I tried to focus on the nude photo of my pregnant mother which hung over the toilet but my hand involuntarily crept towards my sweatpants, through the flap of my boxers. Don't sully this moment I told myself. Go back to your family. Exercise restraint. Respect. Maturity. I imagined the nurse doggie-style and finished in a decorative towel.

When I returned the living room smelled of ammonia and my mom and sister were holding each other crying. The dog murderer was carrying a Cashew-sized bundle out the door. She boarded a sprinter van with my oldest friend. *You're a pervert, you know,* sobbed my sister. I said *yeah* I knew and I thought about two things: The first thing was what if Cashew's heart stopped at the same exact moment I came into the hand towel? Two lives extinguished on polar ends of the cycle. An instance of pleasure and pain, then nothingness. I forgot the second thing I thought about.

Little Dubrovnik

The workers ate their lunches as the Catholic high school let out across the street. They whistled at the girls in pleated skirts and polos who walked by. The girls grouped tighter together, their plaid disguising them like zebra stripes. One dawdled behind the rest and he could feel her watching him. As she walked over the other workers clucked and hollered.

"What's in your sandwich?" she asked him.

The waist of her skirt had been rolled so the hem brushed the tops of her knees.

"Sardines."

He removed the top layer of bread to show her the four perpendicular fish.

"You eat the bones and everything?"

"Yes."

"Can I try?"

He handed her the sandwich. She took a bite and squinted.

She said, "do you know what you're building here?"

"Parking lot."

"For the school," she said. "It's like you're building it for me."

Then she skipped off to catch the bus with her friends. Her keys jingled from where they hung on her backpack.

"Get it, bro," the workers called.

He walked to work in the dark. Past saints in glass cases with fruit offerings at their feet. Past a barefoot man sleeping against a cellphone store. Girls in burkas pushing burlap bags of jasmine rice. Mexican men selling fruit out of carts. Past women listening to Haitian radio and hanging laundry on lines. He clocked in at dawn and unloaded piping from the truck. The men he worked with were older than him. They spoke Spanish and Polish and played cards after work. He walked home in the dark. His room was divided by an accordion wall behind which a Pakistani man mumbled in his sleep.

When he got home that night he listened to kids lighting fireworks outside and counted his money. The next day a worker cut his thumb off with the table saw and the site closed early. He was frustrated to lose the day's work.

The schoolgirl came up to him again the following afternoon and sat down. This time, she said nothing and rifled through her knapsack. She pulled out a sardine sandwich and took a bite. He laughed at her.

"What's your name?" she asked him.

"Luka."

"Where are you from?"

"Croatia."

She nodded. The other girls called for her and she stood up. He sat at eye level with her knees, fine, blonde hair on each.

"What time do you get off?"

She was waiting for him when he clocked out, no longer in her uniform but instead slim-fitting jeans and a sweater with her hair pulled back into twin braids.

"I'm Abigail by the way," she said.

"Yes," he said, pointing to her necklace which read "Abigail" in silver script.

They walked for a block, past a man selling bouquets of roses, a bucket drummer, and a window of chickens strung up by their feet.

"I don't know this neighborhood well," she said.

They walked by a sign reading LIVE NUDE GIRLS GIRLS GIRLS above a dark bar. A pawn shop. An apothecary with bins of dried crickets out front. An emaciated cat eyeing them. They passed through a park with wood chips instead of grass. Several children's birthday parties were wrapping up. Brazilian men offered face painting. They displayed pictures of wolves and dragons and Hello Kitty. She seemed intrigued by this.

"No," Luka insisted.

He searched his mind for the words.

"Face AIDS."

"Face AIDS?"

She offered him her phone and he typed into the translator.

"Oh! Scabies."

"Very dirty."

Luka stopped at a falafel stand where he parted with $7.00 to buy her a kebob. They sat on the curb.

"Beautiful," he said, pointing to her ring.

"It's a mood ring. It changes color depending on what mood I'm in."

"How?"

"Magic."

"No magic."

"Yes magic!"

"You crazy."

Abigail licked the grease from her fingers and unzipped her bag. She pulled out a glass bottle, took a swig, then handed it to Luka. The bottle was shaped like a woman's torso.

"Loša djevojčica."

"What's that mean?"

She hit a vape pen and exhaled a blue cloud.

"Bad little girl."

It started to rain so Luka took her to his apartment. He set her Uggs on the radiator like rotisserie chickens. The room smelled like mildew and curry. The Pakistani man was gone and his bed vacant. Abigail took a faded pencil case out of her knapsack and pulled out an X-acto knife, then her yearbook. She traced the outline of her school photo with the knife, removed it from the book, and handed it to Luka. He put it in the photo sleeve of his wallet, replacing a Dunkin' Donuts punch card.

Luka laid concrete for eleven hours. He coughed little clouds of gray debris like an old furnace. One of the guys dropped a joint into the pour and it became part of the foundation. Part of her parking lot. At home he found that the accordion wall was parted and the other half of the room was now occupied by a one-armed man in combat pants. He was smoking a cigarette and offered one to Luka who accepted. What remained of the man's arm was tattooed with busty mermaids, caressing his stump. He'd hung a picture of Selena Gomez on the wall.

"Let's go to my house," she said, so he followed her.

They took a bus to the north end of the South Bay, a neighborhood where Luka had never been. Her room could swallow his in triplicate. She had shelves of soccer trophies and magazines and purple bedding with tomorrow's uniform pressed and laid out. She flopped down on the bed and beckoned for him to join her.

She told him about a girl at school who loved rabbits so her father bought her the world's largest rabbit. It was monstrous, the size of a great dane. It cost him a million dollars. She was terrified of the thing. They kept it in a stable down the street. Luka said they should have eaten it and Abigail laughed.

She told him that she had these night terrors so her parents sent her to a shrink and the shrink gave her these pills and she poured some out into her hand to show him. They were purple like her mood ring. Like her bedspread. Luka said he'd never been to therapy. His family worked hard and put little emphasis on mental health. But he'd once taken a restorative mineral bath.

She read his tarot, delicately placing ornate cards over one another. When she pulled The Devil he swept the deck off the bed and called her a gypsy. She draped herself over him. He lifted her up and down like a dumbbell.

"Too skinny," he said. "Like starving orphan."

"How long have you been here?" she asked him.

"Two months."

"And you like working construction?"

"S'okay."

"I want to be an actress."

"*You talking to me?*"

"Exactly."

She stroked his head. Traced the bridge of his nose with her finger.

"Do you have Instagram?"

"No phone."

Then Abigail's dad opened the door holding a golf club. He chased Luka into the street. He said he'd seen Luka on the doorbell camera. That if he came around again he'd splatter his skull across the pavement. Abigail didn't pass the site again for a few days.

The one-armed vet was listening to dubstep and doing sit-ups when Luka got home. He counted his money in the bathroom down the hall. When he returned, the vet was making instant noodles on a hot plate.

"Where ya been, man?"

Luka shrugged. He looked over the vet's things. Some

girly magazines and prescription bottles. His pills were purple like Abigail's.

"You got a girl?"

He smiled. Luka handed him Abigail's school photo.

"She's something." The vet opened his own velcro wallet. "I got a girl back home too."

He handed Luka a picture of a Wheaten Terrier.

At lunch he waited for her on the Catholic school steps but the nuns shooed him away. After work Abigail waited for him at the site. A woman in a halter top and heels with a large animal tattoo stood outside smoking and Abigail stood with her, hitting her vape pen, until Luka came out. He put his hard hat on her head.

"I have something for you."

She handed Luka a mini iPhone 7.

"You crazy!"

They walked to the shoreline where black water lapped at the heels of graffitied shipping containers. Signs warned against swimming. The area was contaminated by runoff from the oil refinery, Abigail explained. She took a photo of Luka against the sunset.

"I'm making you an Instagram. What's your full name?"

"Luka Ćiro Blažević."

"How do you spell that?"

The temperature dipped with the sun and Luka wrapped Abigail in his jacket. She felt like nothing. He wanted to feed her a million-dollar rabbit.

She walked to the bus stop. Past telephone poles with flyers for babysitters, cello lessons, and Christian-science church groups. Past women in athleisure pushing double-decker strollers. A park with kids doing live-action role-play, mauling each other with dull weapons. At school she went to the front office and said she needed to change her elective from acting to Croatian. The woman at the front desk told her it was too late in the term to change her elective, and were it not, the school did not offer Croatian. She could take Spanish next semester.

Her third-period teacher announced a canned food drive for the needy. One girl remarked that they should just donate everything to Abigail's boyfriend. Abigail hit the girl in the face with the back of her hand and was suspended for three days. She texted Luka that she would not be able to see him that night.

"What happen?"

"I got in a fight."

"Loša djevojčica."

But she couldn't sleep. Climbing out of the kitchen window bypassed the doorbell camera. She ran across the damp lawn, setting off the neighbor's motion-sensor lights, dodging sprinklers and bougainvillea. They met at the 24-hour McDonald's. Luka asked her what her night terrors were about. She said she couldn't remember. She sipped a strawberry shake and traced patterns in the condensation on the cup's side.

He told her that his family used to fish outside Dubrovnik and his grandparents would make Pijani šaran and gradele and mostaccioli with salmon. The water was clear and blue, not like here. She asked him if he missed it and he said very much. She said hang on and went up to the counter. It was so abrupt, he worried he'd offended her.

"Maybe you can find things here that you like too."

She brought him a Filet-O-Fish.

The night was cold against Abigail's stockings. He chided her for not dressing warmer. They walked into an old church with topiary angels out front. An AA meeting was gathered in the basement and Abigail took two cookies from their table. Mary was depicted in various stages of grief around the altar. They curled up together in a confessional and ate the alcoholics' cookies. She asked if Luka went to church back home. He said they had the most beautiful churches she'd ever seen.

"What happens when the parking lot is done?" she asked.

Luka thought. Mary grieved. The alcoholics said *one day at a time, one day at a time.* They heard sirens passing outside. Luka imagined the police of this neighborhood charging him, all armed with golf clubs. Abigail pressed against his chest where she eventually fell asleep.

They woke up in the light of the booth's latticed screen.

"What happens," she picked up where she'd left off, "when you finish building the parking lot?"

Luke smiled at her. "Build another."

Autofiction

THIS IS MY MAGNUM OPUS. This is everything I've consumed since last Thursday[1]. This is my Facebook password: *IHATECONNORSIMCOX*. Tihs is a medical conidtion taht I hvae[2]. I don't remember where I was

---

1 unripe banana / b 12 multivitamin / sweetgreen green goddess salad / trail mix / half avocado / boxed wine product / 75mg effexor / birth control / peach / apple and almond butter / salmon cut roll / 75mg effexor / birth control / oatmeal / coffee / thai food / 5 cigarettes / 4 olives / 2 martinis / 1g cocaine divided amongst 6 people / 4 oysters / 75mg effexor / birth control / yogurt / veggie burger / coffee / trail mix (only the chocolate) / .5mg ativan / mediterranean fusion bowl / some loose slices of cheese / 75mg effexor / birth control / gluten free muffin / artichoke hearts / salad with mom at stanley's / no birth control shit / coffee i made with complicated machine at work / overly ripe banana

2 **Dyslexia**, also known as reading disorder, is a disorder characterized by reading below the expected level for their age. Different people are affected to different degrees. Problems may include difficulties in spelling words, reading quickly, writing words, "sounding out" words in the head, pronouncing words when reading aloud and understanding what one reads.

when this happened[3]. This is the last thing my stepmother tweeted: *Enjoy your memorial day and remember all those who made the ultimate sacrifice so we could spend the day as free Americans* 🇺🇸. I went to Lutheran school and remember this bible verse: *For God so loved the world that he gave his only begotten Son, that whoever believes in him shall not perish but have eternal life.* Here it is poorly translated into Coratian: Jer Bog je tako ljubio svijet da je dao svoga Sina Jedinorođenca da nijedan koji u njega vjeruje ne propadne, nego da ima život vječni. This is the definition of the word begotten: *brought into existence.* This is something I learned from the movie Jurassic Park: life finds a way.

This Is A List Of People Who Appear in this Book
Madeline
Elijah
Anika
Jake Willner
Katja
Blake
Abigail
Xian
Laura Cohen
Pablo
Dorian
Max
Walker
Zoe
Lauren Myracle

---

3 The September 11 attacks, commonly referred to as 9/11 were a series of four coordinated suicide terrorist attacks by the militant Islamist terrorist network al-Qaeda against the United States on Tuesday September 11, 2001.

Mr. Hayworth
Dante
Lacey McKelvy
Hannah
Nick
Dominic
Mark
Sophia
Steph
Rachel
Bradford
Shara
Gracie
Cashew
Jude Thomas
Ben Sharlack
Al Friedman
Lucien
Luka Ćiro Blažević

Some of these people are real and some are canceled and some of them are dead and some of them have drinking problems and some I met at Christian Surf Camp and one of them had scabies.

This Is How I Was Sent To Christian Surf Camp

I was sent to Christian Surf Camp after this girl[4] and I took her dad's car for a joy ride. We were twelve so we

---

4 Victoria Dawn Justice is an American actress, singer-songwriter, and dancer, who is best known for her roles as Lola Martinez in the Nickelodeon sitcom Zoey 101 from 2006 to 2008 and as Tori Vega in Victorious from 2010 to 2013.

weren't considered legal drivers in the state of California. She rear-ended another car because her feet didn't fully reach the pedals. We left the scene of the accident but not before the car got our license plate. The cops showed up later that night to bust the perps but the perps were two twelve-year-old girls in Hello Kitty sleeping bags. So I was sent to Christian Surf Camp where I went on a hunger strike and Victoria came out with this music video[5] about driving in America. While on my hunger strike I felt like Gandhi and realized that if you martyr yourself long enough you actually start to believe in whatever it is you're advocating for.

This Is How Elijah's Girlfriend Committed Vehicular Manslaughter

Elijah brought the scabies. Elijah brought the scabies from Bard > Sarah Lawrence > downtown Manhattan. Elijah started a transatlantic scabies pipeline. Elijah also brought this pretty Colombian girl whom he was dating at the time. She was quiet but when she got drunk she told Elijah something. She told Elijah that once she hit a hitchhiker while she was driving on a dark road in Colombia. She just kept driving and then came to America for boarding school and then to Bard College and then got drunk and told Elijah. Elijah held her and comforted her and pet her hair and told her it was alright and itched his back where skin mites were silently gorging on his flesh.

---

5 Victorious Cast - Make It In America (Official Video) ft. Victoria Justice

AUTOFICTION

これは京都です

A Japanese man at a bar said he'd pay me ¥30,000 for the majority of my hair. He handed me a pair of scissors and told me to go to the bathroom and cut off my ponytail and then fanned the bills out in his hands. I had never traded my hair as currency and therefore didn't know what it was worth but decided to take the deal because I was broke and abroad and thought it might make good fodder for this story. In the bathroom I snipped off my ponytail at the nape of my neck with the man's scissors which I realized he carried around with him. I came back into the bar holding my ponytail like a dead squirrel. The man was gone. I carried my hair home on the train. Another American girl got on the train a few stops after me. She had puffy eyes like she'd been crying. She was also holding a ponytail.

This Is The Plot Of *Jurassic Park*

Alan Grant alongside Laura Dern and Jeff Goldblum visit an island theme park run by disgraced scientist Richard Attenborough, who has reanimated and plans to profit off of dinosaurs. These two children[6] come as well and this is the pinnacle of their acting careers. The dinosaurs inevitably free themselves from their feeble restraints and wreak havoc on the island and its inhabitants. Casualties include Samuel L. Jackson, the lawyer, the Australian guy and the fat Jimmy Buffett guy who played Newman in Seinfeld. The movie's refrain, *life finds a way*, reminds us that, in the battle between man and nature, the latter will

6 'Jurassic Park' Child Stars Joseph Mazzello and Ariana Richards Are Open to Reprising Their Roles (Exclusive), ET, 2019

always prevail. At its core, Jurassic Park is about a child-hesitant paleontologist who, over two hours and seven minutes, warms to the idea of fatherhood. This aspect of the film above all, is unrealistic. I watched Jurassic Park bi-weekly from the ages of eight to eleven and again recently in a hotel room while my boyfriend did ketamine off a mirrored tray. I ranted about the seminal moment when Jurassic Park entered my life and how Richard Attenborough, like my father, was a market capitalist bulldozing forward without considering consequence. And then my boyfriend asked me if I thought there was any validity to that conspiracy about tap water causing infertility. And I steered the conversation back to Jurassic Park like, "just because we *can* do something doesn't mean we *should*." And he said I *should* probably reconsider drinking tap water and water in general if I ever want to conceive and I said we were doing drugs we'd purchased from a man named SL33T so comparatively the damage from tap water was negligible. My boyfriend ate Jordan almonds from the mini fridge, which an itemized receipt later revealed were $500. Then we took a bubble bath because it was our anniversary or birthday or the Chinese New Year or something that warranted a celebration. And I thought *how can I take a bubble bath in this fine hotel and still be so miserable?* Life finds a way. I was leading the league in misery. My shrink said it was chemical. Prescribed me Effexor. Recommended exercise and charged me an uninsured rate. I said to my boyfriend, "I feel like there is something poisoning my brain. Something I can't even see." And my boyfriend said, "Yeah. It's chemicals in the tap water." He asked me to tell him a story and I told him about the time a Japanese man bought my hair.

This Is A Photo Of A Black Hole

This is a photo of a black hole. It's the best photo of a black hole ever taken, not from an artistic perspective but from a scientific one. It looks like the camera misfired, only capturing the end of a cigarette. Blink and you'll miss the black hole. But in reality it is the begotten soul of the universe, simultaneously letting us view our past and our future, and no one, artist nor scientist, knows where it leads.

About the author

Madeline Cash is a copywriter from California.
She founded and edits Forever Magazine.

Previously Published

- "Little Dubrovnik" originally published in Carve, 2023
- "The Jester's Privilege" published by Joyland, 2023
- "Plagues" originally published in The Drunken Canal, 2022 / reissued in Electric Literature 2023
- "Hollywood Tours" originally published in The Drift, 2022
- "Fortune Teller" originally published in Terror House, 2022
- "Sponge Cake" originally published in Muumuu House, 2022
- "Autofiction" Originally published in Blue Arrangements, 2022
- "Slumber Party" originally published in The Baffler, 2021
- "They Ate the Children First" originally published in Hobart, 2021
- "Good Boy" published by Forever Mag, 2021
- "Beauty Queen" originally published in Ligeia Mag, 2021
- "Hostage #4" originally published in The Literary Review, 2020
- "Earth Angel" originally published in Always Crashing, 2020
- "Mark's Turtles" abridged version published in Expat, 2020
- "TGIF" originally published in Peach Mag, 2020
- "Little Dalmatia" published in KGB Lit, 2020

ALSO BY CLASH BOOKS

GAG REFLEX
Elle Nash

WHAT ARE YOU
Lindsay Lerman

HEXIS
Charlene Elsby

LIFE OF THE PARTY
Tea Hacic

GIRL LIKE A BOMB
Autumn Christian

INTERNET GIRLFRIEND
Stephanie Valente

FABLES OF THE DECONSTRUCTION
Damian Dressick

DON'T PUSH THE BUTTON
John Skipp

THE PUSSY DETECTIVE
DuVay Knox

WE PUT THE LIT IN LITERARY
clashbooks.com

 @clashbooks  @clashbooks /clashbooks

Email
clashmediabooks@gmail.com